LAWS OF WITCHCRAFT

The Uncensored Memoirs of a Book Hunter
Book 1

C.J. ARCHER

Copyright © 2026 by C.J. Archer

Visit C.J. at www.cjarcher.com

All rights reserved.

No part of this book may be reproduced in any form or by any electronic or mechanical means, including information storage and retrieval systems, without written permission from the author, except for the use of brief quotations in a book review.

INTRODUCTION

Dear Reader,

    A good book has the power to transport. A great book can be life-changing. I do not claim that my memoir is such a book, but I do hope you'll understand by the end how the adventures I recount—of which this is the first—changed me.

    As I sit down to write this memoir in 1920, I am taken back to the disruptive days of the early 1890s, when the world first learned of the existence of magicians, forced into hiding for centuries. Laws were introduced to end their persecution. New commercial opportunities arose. Lives and livelihoods changed for so many, both magicians and the artless. From the ashes of those transformative days emerged a bold idea, much like the magicians themselves: a public library stocked with important works on magic, sourced from every corner of the earth. Its purpose

INTRODUCTION

was to strengthen our vague understanding of magic, so that everyone who wished to study it might do so.

It is with that in mind that Oscar Barratt and I took on the task of finding relevant material.

In each volume of these memoirs, I recount the acquisition of a significant work that is now housed in the Glass Library collection, located on Crooked Lane, London. As you will discover, some journeys were quite an experience! Oscar and I encountered extraordinary people, most of them agreeable, but not all. I'd like to point out that any opinions expressed in these memoirs about them are my own, and do not reflect those of Oscar, unless stated otherwise.

Finally, I have done my best to recreate the events as they unfolded, including accounts of private conversations, intimate details of our lives, and my innermost thoughts. These volumes are uncensored to give you, dear reader, a more complete picture of our adventures. An edited version suitable for public consumption may come later at the behest of others but, for now, I will leave these very personal parts in.

I hope you enjoy the first volume of *The Uncensored Memoirs of a Book Hunter*.

~ Professor Gavin Nash

CHAPTER 1

SUMMER 1893

"Lady Coyle's son looks remarkably like her coachman."

I always thought I'd begin my memoir with a profound statement, one that made readers wonder at my insightfulness and marvel at my wit. But, given how the rest of this chronicle turned out, it seemed more appropriate to start with that line of dialog, spoken by my friend and fellow book collector, Oscar Barratt.

"Did you hear me, Gavin?" he asked. "Or are you declining to respond because your professorial temperament places you above gossip?"

I shushed him with a finger to my lips then pointed at the closed door. "She may be just on the other side."

"I doubt it, but if she is, she won't hear a thing. That door is solid as rock."

Oscar stood with hands on hips as he scanned the book spines on one of the library shelves in Lady Coyle's

Belgravia townhouse. It was a small room with space for only one armchair, a well-worn brown leather wingback angled toward the clean fireplace. Floor-to-ceiling bookshelves lined two of the walls and a painting of a bucolic country scene hung above the mantelpiece. It was warm and inviting, and not at all like the library's former owner, the late Lord Coyle. His widow, Hope, Lady Coyle, was equally cold.

Oscar's reassurance that we couldn't be overheard gave me the confidence to press him further about his scandalous declaration. "You don't think Coyle fathered the boy before his death?"

Oscar looked at me like I was a naive fool. Sometimes I felt like one, particularly with him. I may be a professor of history and a few years older, but Oscar possessed a worldliness that made him much wiser than me in many respects. "I believe in magic, not miracles. The child was born ten months *after* the death of Lord Coyle. As if that wasn't enough, he has red hair like the coachman."

"Coyle could have had red hair once." The earl had been aged in his sixties when he died over a year ago. What little hair had clung to his head had been white at the time.

Oscar smirked, lending him a rakish air. He cut a striking figure with a short goatee beard and dark brown hair that could do with a trim as it curled around his ears. His eyes were equally dark, and often reflected his mood. I used to feel self-conscious in his company. My thinning hair, slim frame and spectacles marked me as the mediocre one against his heroic good looks, but I never felt jealous of him. Oscar was simply too good-natured to invoke envy.

That friendliness coupled with his handsome looks meant the women brazenly flirted with him. Not that he seemed to notice. Or perhaps he just didn't care. For much of the three years I'd known him, Oscar had been bitter after his relationship with Lady Louisa Hollingbroke ended, and that seemed to have colored his interactions with the fairer sex. Lately, however, since we'd made up our minds to undertake our first journey, his sense of humor had returned. He smiled more and seemed positive about the future. Considering we were about to embark on an adventure together, it was a relief. I hadn't relished spending every day with a melancholic companion.

I stood alongside him and studied the book spines, too. Where to begin? The collection of the late Lord Coyle wasn't vast, but his widow had given us free rein to take whichever titles appealed to us; for a price, of course. Closer inspection proved not many were on the subject that interested us. Magic. That was surprising, considering Lord Coyle was an avid collector of magical objects. It seemed his interest didn't extend to books *about* magic.

We began plucking tomes off the shelves and reading a few pages to gauge their relevance. Lord Coyle's collection would hopefully provide a solid base on which to build a library about magic on behalf of Matt and India Glass—now Lord and Lady Rycroft—who were partly funding it. After we acquired as many books as we could from Lady Coyle, Oscar and I planned to travel the world in search of others. The problem was, we didn't know where to begin. The world was rather large.

Oscar's sharp intake of breath, followed by the sound of wood scraping on the floorboards, had me looking up from the book I was studying. A panel of the bookshelves had opened like a door to reveal a secret room beyond.

Oscar and I exchanged wide-eyed glances. Then he grinned like a naughty schoolboy before squeezing into the room. It was no larger than a cupboard and packed with odds and ends. There were quite a few sculptures and paintings, a brass candelabra, pieces of porcelain, boxes of various shapes, a dining chair, cloths, jewelry, and even stuffed animals. It was an eclectic collection, with no theme tying it all together. Or so it seemed to me.

Oscar picked up a white plate with a decorative blue border then put it down again without taking a closer look. Next, he picked up a stuffed hawk with its wings spread, then returned it to the pedestal. He touched the marble stand itself, running his fingers down the column as if reading its veins like braille.

"Magic," he declared. "All of it."

So, this was Lord Coyle's elusive collection of magical objects. I'd heard India mention it, but had never seen it. As a magician himself, Oscar could feel magic that had been placed into an object, even if it wasn't his discipline of ink. For ink that did contain magic, the power called to him in a way an attractive woman draws the gaze of men. As an artless, I felt no such compulsion toward anything in particular in the storeroom, although the space itself intrigued me.

"I do love a hidden room in a library," I murmured.

Oscar wasn't listening. His face was a picture of rapture as he traced the title of a book with his fingertip, as if he could feel the strokes of the pen that had formed it. It was handwritten, the spine damaged, and it required careful handling or it would fall apart. Oscar was gentle, putting my mind at ease.

"*Monsters and Myths of the Central American Tribes,*" I read. "It sounds intriguing, but it doesn't fit our criteria." The library we were creating would house the world's greatest collection of books, essays, letters *et cetera* about magic, past and present. "Books about fantastical creatures are just that—fantasy," I told him.

He spoke some words in another language. They had a poetic rhythm to them, the syllables undulating as they rolled off his tongue, like gentle waves lapping at the shoreline.

The words on the title page rose in the air, leaving behind a blank page. Like autumn leaves in a breeze, they slowly floated around the room, drifting so close to my face I could smell the ink. With a few more words, Oscar picked up the pace and jumbled the letters up before gently placing them back on the page in their correct order.

He smiled at me. "Ink magic." Not only could he sense ink magic, he could also manipulate ink in a pretty fashion. If he manufactured it, he could make sure it didn't fade for a very long time, but he'd left the family manufacturing business when he moved to London to pursue a career in journalism.

"Oscar," I gently chided. "The library is for books *about* magic, not books that *contain* it." I plucked it from his hands, intending to put it back.

Two sheets of paper slipped out from between the pages and fluttered to the floor. He picked them up and read. "Well, well. How intriguing. These are letters. Coyle must have placed them in that monster book for safekeeping, as they seem to have nothing to do with it. One is from a Scotsman named Kinloch. He seems to know Coyle, but there's no love lost between them. He states that he won't sell his book to Coyle, 'not now, not ever'. The whole tone is terse." He handed the letter to me. "Note the title of the book mentioned."

"*A Treatise on the Laws of Witchcraft and Maleficium in Scotland* by His Majesty's Lord Advocate George Mackenzie."

My pulse quickened. I'd heard of the book in my scholarly endeavors, but never seen a copy. Indeed, there were few known copies in existence. Such a rare tome would be a worthy addition to our library.

Magicians were denounced as evil by many societies in the distant past. A plethora of documentation existed about the persecution of magicians that led to many being put to death. Others hid their magic and forced their descendants to do the same, so eventually the artless forgot about them. Sorcery faded from the collective conscience, becoming legend, until quite recently. As with many of the past's shameful events, women bore the brunt of the persecution. In this instance, female magicians were labeled as witches.

It was a pity Kinloch never sold the book to Coyle. If he had, it would now be in our hands.

"I never learned Latin," Oscar said, somewhat apologetically. "What does *maleficium* mean?"

"Harmful magic," I said. "And a lord advocate is the chief public prosecutor. I've studied George Mackenzie, as it happens."

"For your lessons at University College?"

"For pleasure in my spare time."

Oscar's lips twitched with his smile.

I stiffened. "Not everyone is inclined to carouse all night with wine, women and song, thank you."

"If you think my life has been one long party, you're sorely mistaken. Any time I spent carousing was part of a concerted effort to further my journalism career. It just so happens that newspaper editors like to drink. A lot. There wasn't much time left over for learning Latin and reading up on obscure Scottish lawyers."

"Point taken, but Mackenzie isn't obscure. He's the most well-known lord advocate, a position he held for a number of years from 1677. He labeled the punishments meted out to convicted witches cruel. He conducted extensive research into witches and concluded that most of the time, their craft was medicinal, not magical. His work led to the abolition of witchcraft trials in Scotland. The rest of the world eventually followed."

"Quite an enlightened man for the seventeenth century. But you said 'most.'"

"Pardon?"

"'He concluded that *most* of the time, a witch's craft was medicinal, not magical.' Are you saying he also found *some* evidence of real magic?"

I shrugged. "It's a question that scholars with an interest in the occult have often wondered, but only amongst ourselves. To discuss such things in mainstream circles would have been career suicide. Anyway, without evidence, the discussions were inconclusive."

Oscar studied the second letter. "Perhaps the book in Kinloch's possession will lay the question to rest once and for all." The somewhat absent note in his voice intrigued me.

"What does the second letter say? Is it also from Kinloch?"

He folded the letter and shook his head. "It's from John J. Defoe."

"The American railroad magnate? What does he say?"

Oscar hesitated before passing me the letter.

I unfolded it and read. It was clearly the first time Defoe had corresponded with Lord Coyle. Written almost five years ago, he introduced himself as a fellow collector of magic. He'd heard about a book that gave a clue to the whereabouts of another text that he sought. The book containing the clue was titled *A Treatise on the Laws of Witchcraft and Maleficium in Scotland*. Defoe didn't know where to find it, however, so he appealed to Lord Coyle.

While that was intriguing, it was the next lines that caught my attention. Now I understood Oscar's hesitation in handing the letter to me. There must be a part of him that wanted to keep the information to himself. To his credit, he had not.

Defoe's ultimate aim was to find a text about tattoos made with magic ink that could turn the tattooed person into a superior human. "How extraordinary. Have you heard of tattoo magic?"

Oscar's eyes were bright, as if he were in the throes of a feverish delirium. "No, but it makes sense that it exists. Tattoos are made with ink, and magic ink in the skin can potentially have a number of practical applications. Superior strength, or perhaps even make the person fly."

I laughed, but he looked quite serious.

"If I can make regular ink fly, why not a tattoo? And if the tattoo is within the skin itself, then why not the human?" He clasped my elbow. "Gavin, we *have* to get that text about tattoo magic."

His enthusiasm didn't surprise me, given he was an ink magician, but I was more intrigued by the book containing the clue. *A Treatise on the Laws of Witchcraft and Maleficium in Scotland* by His Majesty's Lord Advocate George Mackenzie could be an important historical document, something we academics referred to as seminal.

"We don't know if Coyle wrote back to Defoe and mentioned that Kinloch has Mackenzie's book," I warned him. "If he did, it could now be in Defoe's possession. I suppose we could make him an offer."

Oscar scoffed. "Coyle would never help a fellow collector. He was too selfish."

"Even if Mr. Kinloch does still have it, what if he doesn't want to sell?" I indicated the first letter where he stated as much.

"He didn't want to sell to *Coyle*. We are not him. In fact, we hated him. Perhaps Kinloch would be prepared to negotiate with his enemy's enemy."

The sound of light footsteps approaching silenced me before I could respond. Lady Coyle stopped at the entrance to the hidden storeroom and gawped in an unladylike fashion at our surroundings. "Well," she said on a breath. "You've found his collection."

Oscar showed her one of the books on the library shelf. "I pulled on this and the hidden door opened."

She picked up a pair of silver earrings inlaid with blue enamel that matched her eyes. "I suppose most of this is worthless, now that magic is no longer a secret. He used to hoard it in the hope the value would rise, but India and Matt's actions sank it instead."

"I doubt that was their motive for liberating magicians from persecution," Oscar said wryly.

Hope cast him a frosty glare that lasted a mere moment before warming. She clasped his arm with both hands and blinked up at him. She was quite beautiful, although I'd heard one of her sisters rejoice that Hope had put on weight during her pregnancy. Oscar showed no sign of discomfort at her flirtation. He was capable of fending off unwanted attentions, and I was quite sure that in this case, they were indeed unwanted. I was glad she focused only on him and ignored me. She was like a tropical jellyfish; beautiful and elegant to the point of mesmerizing, but capable of stinging those who got too close. I'd learned to stay silent in her company and let Oscar do all the talking.

This was the second time Oscar and I had met her in as many weeks. We'd had unpleasant dealings with her before, of course, but those turbulent times were now behind us. We were moving forward, as was the entire country. It was time for magicians like Oscar to come out of the shadows and take advantage of the freedom afforded to them under new legislation that forbade their persecution.

He was precisely the sort of man to take advantage, too. Enthusiastic, enterprising, and forthright, with a thirst for knowledge and adventure. He'd been chomping at the bit for over a year, eager to begin our book-gathering expeditions. Our visit to Lady Coyle was the first such expedition. Since the Coyle townhouse was based in London and the widow eager to sell as many of her late husband's books as possible, it seemed like the easiest place to start. Besides, we had no other specific destinations in mind yet, just vague notions of visiting the continent.

"Are you interested in buying any of the books, Oscar?" she purred.

Oscar smoothly extricated himself from her grip in such a way that it didn't appear as though he were rejecting her outright. "We've made a collection on the table." He placed *Monsters and Myths of the Central Amer-*

ican Tribes on top of the pile. "Is there a footman who can help us with these? And can your butler fetch us a cab?"

"I no longer employ a butler, but my coachman can take you wherever you wish to go."

A few minutes later, we saw the coachman walking down the main staircase to the entrance hall where we waited. Both Oscar and I stared as he approached, but not entirely because seeing an outside servant inside the house was a rare event. He was indeed a redheaded fellow, just as Oscar had claimed. He was lanky, freckly, and younger than Hope. He also smelled faintly of baby powder. She gave him instructions to bring the carriage around and he hurried to do her bidding. It would seem that, after Lord Coyle, she'd been keen to take a younger, more malleable lover. If the rumors were true, perhaps she hadn't waited for her husband's death.

As we drove away from the townhouse where so much drama had occurred last year, Oscar patted the crate of books beside him. "So, what do you think?"

"I think with her looks and the money her son inherited, she'll find herself another husband quickly, despite her waspish nature. Although I'm not sure she'd want to marry again. I can see her enjoying widowhood and all the benefits that come with being wealthy, clever and attractive."

Oscar grinned. "Not quite the vague professor you appear to be, are you?"

"Vague?"

"But I wasn't asking for your thoughts on Lady Coyle. I meant what do you think of our purchases?"

"I'm pleased with our haul. It's a good beginning."

"Indeed. May I look at the letters that fell out of the book about monsters?"

"I left them behind," I said. "I didn't think we needed them, and we'd only agreed to the books. Taking them would be theft."

He looked disappointed. "The title of the book owned by Kinloch was long. I can't remember it. Nor can I recall his address."

"I've memorized both."

He flashed a smile. "Good man. I knew that prodigious memory of yours would come in handy."

I didn't think my memory was all that special, but I liked that he thought it was. "We should speak to the Glasses about funds and check the railway timetable. We can travel to Scotland this week."

"You mean Lord and lady Rycroft."

I often forgot the formal titles of the easygoing India and Matthew Glass. Their lack of pretense was what made them such delightful company. "I believe they're all currently in London."

"All? As in Lord and Lady Rycroft, the baby, and the members of their entourage?"

"And the newlyweds who live here," I added. "Do you know, I never thought Willie would go through with it. She doesn't seem like the marrying kind."

He chuckled. "Shall we make a wager on how long the marriage will last?"

"Oscar! You can't do that. Besides, I doubt Detective Inspector Brockwell would divorce her. He seems like a steady fellow who'd follow through on a promise until the end."

"Who says it will end in divorce? Or that he'll be the one to end it?"

I pushed my glasses up my nose. "That's a rather cynical view of things. Willie may be volatile, but I truly believe she loves him."

He turned to look out of the window, but I doubt his distant gaze took in any of the streetscape. "Marriage has nothing to do with love, apparently."

Poor Oscar. Although he'd been the one to end their relationship, Lady Louisa had given him no choice after he realized she only wanted to marry him because he was a magician. Oscar wanted to be loved and to love in return. She'd wanted to be the mother of magician children and hadn't particularly cared who fathered them.

His cynical declaration about love and marriage was proof he must still be struggling to move on from his ill-fated romance, despite outward appearances. The more I got to know Oscar, the more I'd come to realize he wasn't as cavalier as he liked everyone to believe.

CHAPTER 2

I was used to seeing Matt and India's Park Street residence full to the brim. Their friends and family members often stayed there, but now the babies made it seem even fuller. The inquisitive minds of little Gabriel Glass and Alexander Bailey sent them wobbling off on chubby legs as soon as their parents' backs were turned. Small fingers found their way under sofas, inside vases, and twisted in the fringes of the rug. If they couldn't see what was on a table, they reached up anyway and grasped whatever they could touch. At one point, Gabriel managed to climb onto an armchair then helped his slightly younger friend up by hauling on an arm and then a leg. The boys looked rather pleased with themselves. The adults in the room commented on how adorable they both were, then fell into conversations about other things. With the attention no longer on them, Alexander grasped

Willie's brandy glass from the nearby table and sipped while Gabriel bit down on one of her cigars. Both boys spat out their mouthfuls onto the carpet after discovering the tastes not to their liking.

"Willie!" India cried as she scooped up the mess with a cloth she kept at hand. "Have you not learned to keep things out of their reach?"

"It ain't my fault they want to try all my favorite vices." Willie tousled the tuft of dark hair on Gabriel's head. "Just wait until you're older, young man. I'll take you to the racetrack, dockside taverns, and..." Her gaze flicked to India and Matt, standing side by side with matching scowls for Matt's irresponsible cowgirl cousin. Willie bent and whispered something in baby Gabriel's ear.

He gurgled in response before slipping off the armchair, feet first and backwards, Alexander right behind him.

Catherine Bailey intercepted her son while her husband, Cyclops, gathered Gabriel into his arms before both boys had a chance to escape from the sitting room. Gabriel tried to remove the patch covering Cyclops's damaged eye, but the big man distracted him by tickling his tummy.

Catherine tried to hand Alexander to me, but I backed away. "No, no. You keep him. I'm not very good with babies. Send them to me when they're older and I'll teach them all about the history of magic. Until then, I'll admire their energy from afar."

Alexander wriggled and his mother had trouble

holding him. She was tall, slim and terribly pretty. Both she and her friend, India, were lovely inside and out. Their husbands were lucky men, and both knew it, going by the soft gazes they bestowed on their wives when they thought no one was watching.

I'd thought Willie would be like me and prefer to have nothing to do with the babies, but she proved me wrong. She put her hands out and accepted Alexander from Catherine. Tucking him under one arm, she held him firmly against her side, like a keg of beer, then asked for Gabriel. Cyclops handed him to her, and she tucked the second child under her other arm. Then she whisked them around the room, making whooshing noises as she swooped them up and down like birds flying through the air. The boys squealed with delight.

"You should have one of your own," Matt told her, smirk firmly in place. "I'd wager Brockwell wants children."

"You wash your mouth out, Matthew Glass," she said without breaking stride. "I want to be the fun older cousin, not the boring mother."

Duke, who'd remained silent as he watched the exchange from where he stood by the window, snorted. "The *much* older cousin, you mean."

Willie suddenly stopped to glare at him. "I ain't talking to you."

"Seems to me that you are," Duke drawled in an American accent that was as thick as Willie's and Cyclops's.

She pulled a face then set the boys down on the floor. "You're dead to me, Duke."

"Good. That'll make it easier for both of us when I leave. No unnecessary tears and long farewells."

"Tears? From me? Ha! I'll be throwing your luggage onto the boat as fast as I can."

"You're coming to the port to see me off? Seems you do care, despite the show you're putting on for everyone else's benefit."

"It ain't a show." Willie pointed at her own face. "This is me not caring what you do with the rest of your life. You go on home to America, find a little wife, have some brats and raise horses. I'll take care of everyone here, because I don't abandon my family and friends."

Cyclops spread his arms out wide. "*I'm* staying, too, and I can look after everyone better than you, Willie, now that I'm in the police force."

Willie ignored him. She only had eyes for the stocky figure of Duke, her long-time friend who'd decided to return to his homeland. Willie wasn't yet used to the idea. Going by her antagonistic reaction, I suspected she'd be angry with him for a long time, despite pretending to be unfazed.

"Don't expect me to write," she went on.

"I won't," Duke said. "Your handwriting's illegible anyway."

She thrust her hands on her hips and jutted her chin forward. "And don't expect to come back, either. Once you're gone, you're gone."

"Willie," Matt chided. "Duke will always be welcome here. If you miss him, perhaps you can visit him when he's settled."

Willie wrinkled her nose. "Why would I, when he's dead to me?"

India wrapped her arm around Willie's waist. "You'll regret it if you continue to talk to him in this manner. Be happy for him, as he is for you. You've got Brockwell now, and Cyclops has Catherine, and Matt has me. Let Duke have his turn."

Her lower lip trembled before she bit it. "Why can't he have his turn here in England?"

"Because I want to go home," Duke said, his tone gentler.

She sniffed, turning her face away.

"There's a month before he leaves," Matt said. "Plenty of time for you to get used to the idea, Willie."

"Used to it? Ha!"

"Why don't the two of you go out tonight and discuss it."

Willie lifted her chin even further. "Nope. I told you, he's dead to me."

Duke rolled his eyes. "We'll have a few drinks, find some trouble... It'll be just like old times."

"Not too much trouble," India added.

Willie wiped her nose with the back of her hand. "I s'pose we could get drunk together so you can see what you'll be missing. By the end of the night, I reckon you'll change your mind about leaving me."

Duke's lips twitched as he tried not to smile. "I don't want to get arrested, so we better behave."

"Naw, no need to worry. I'm married to a policeman, so he can get me out."

"Again," Matt muttered.

Catherine gazed proudly at Cyclops. "My husband can also help, now that he's moving up the ranks."

Cyclops, however, didn't hear her. He was too busy looking down at the floor, all around. "Did anyone see where the boys went?"

He, Catherine, Duke and Willie hurried from the room, leaving me alone with Matt and India for the first time since my arrival. India, however, was a little distracted by the disappearance of her son, until Matt's fingers brushed against hers to get her attention.

"They've got it under control," he said.

She leaned into him, a soft smile on her lips. "I know. Do you think it's safe to have Bristow send in refreshments if Mrs. Bristow distracts the boys in the kitchen while we chat to Professor Nash?"

Matt rang for tea then they sat on the sofa, inviting me to sit on one of the armchairs. With the chaos of the babies crawling on the floor, nobody had yet taken a seat.

"You seemed enthusiastic when you arrived," Matt said. "Does that mean you were successful at Hope's library?"

I pushed my glasses up my nose. "Indeed we were. Oscar is unpacking the crate of books at his flat as we speak."

"Anything in particular catch your eye?"

"Not so much a book, but a letter. Two, in fact." I told them about the Scotsman named Kinloch who'd refused to sell a particular book to Lord Coyle, and the American railroad magnate who'd also wanted it. "It's a treatise written by Scotland's Lord Advocate, George Mackenzie, on the laws in that country relating to witch trials. He was an important figure at the time, and his work led to the abolition of witchcraft trials around the world. The book will be a worthy addition to our library. *Your* library."

"It won't belong to us," Matt said.

India regarded me with those warm gray eyes of hers. She seemed to be trying to work something out. Indeed, she appeared to be trying to work something out about *me*. "That's all very interesting, professor, but that's not the entire reason you want the book, is it?"

I cleared my throat. "It's the reason *I* want it. Oscar wants it for a different reason, as does the American, John J. Defoe. According to his letter to Lord Coyle, *A Treatise on the Laws of Witchcraft and Maleficium in Scotland* mentions the location of another text. That text supposedly tells of an ink magic spell that can give the tattooed person the ability to fly."

They blinked back at me with twin expressions of disbelief.

"You look as skeptical as I am," I said.

"You don't believe such a thing is possible?" India asked.

I hesitated, carefully considering my answer. "I'd say the spell has been lost centuries ago."

"But you believe it was possible, once?"

I paused again. We were heading into peculiar territory, and I didn't want to sound like a madman who ought to be committed to Bedlam. But these two were clear-minded, practical folk who'd seen more peculiar things than me. If anyone understood, it would be them. "Do you recall the myths about magic?"

They both nodded, but it was Matt who responded. "Where maps supposedly came to life, causing rivers to flow off the edges and into the real world, or the tentacles of monsters drawn on the maps of oceans reached out of the paper and pulled real ships under the waves."

"Not just maps," India added. "And not just myths. Flying carpets are certainly real, as are giant pyramids, and possibly a watering system that could turn a desert into a lush garden."

It was wonderful to discuss such things with clever, inquisitive people. They were the perfect couple to be patrons of the new library. It ought to be named after them. "If this tattoo ink magic spell existed at some point, it may have been so rare and old by the time of Mackenzie's writing that many dismissed it as legend, just like flying carpets were dismissed. Or, it could be like the map magic, which I suspect is merely legend and was never actually possible."

The butler entered carrying a tray with teapot, cups and saucers. Somewhere in the depths of the house, one of the boys gave an excited exclamation. Neither event distracted India as she continued to give me her full attention. "Either way, it's an intriguing mystery, and I do so love a good mystery."

Matt chuckled. "I take it you're going to call on the owner of the Mackenzie book and offer to buy it off him for the library?"

"We are," I said. "We hope to leave as soon as possible."

India handed me a delicate china teacup that I'd once been told the manufacturer had used his magic to strengthen. "You and Oscar must dine with us before you leave. We'll give you some funds for the journey and send you on your way with a hearty meal."

"I'll let Oscar know," I said.

"Is he looking forward to the journey?"

"Very much. I believe the adventure will do him good."

She frowned as she passed me the silver sugar bowl. "Is he still upset about Lady Louisa? I heard she got married to a carpenter magician, much to the surprise of Matt's aunts."

"Shocking, I think is how they put it," Matt said. "Aunt Letitia was concerned for the health of Louisa's elderly aunt after hearing of her niece's downfall, as she put it, at marrying an ordinary man. My Aunt Beatrice laughed quite cruelly until her youngest daughter, my cousin Charity, declared she thought marrying a carpenter sounded amusing and where could she find one of her own."

Matt's extended family had always been an, er, eclectic

group. Charity in particular had an eccentric streak that could sometimes be cruel. I refrained from commenting and answered India's question. "Oscar hides it well, but I think he is upset. Not that he is still in love with Louisa. I don't believe he ever was. I simply think his experience soured him on relationships altogether. I suspect he plans to stay a bachelor for the rest of his life."

"Ha!" Matt barked.

His wife arched her brows at him in question.

He gave her a lazy smile. "You know as well as I do, my dearest, that sometimes that kind of plan goes awry."

She returned his smile with a secretive one of her own.

I cleared my throat to remind them they weren't alone. "Oscar's focus now is on acquiring books and having adventures, not settling down."

They both gave me indulgent looks. I felt as though I was misunderstanding something, as if they shared a joke where the punchline made sense to them alone. That was the thing about couples. They had a secret language that others didn't understand. Part of me wished I could be understood to such a degree by another.

But mostly I was just glad I could pursue my interests without having to answer to anyone else. No wife would allow me to leave my safe career as a professor of history to go traveling the world to indulge my interest in obscure, old books.

For the first time since making the decision, I felt utterly confident about it. I knew deep in my bones that it was the right course to take, that the path I was about to embark upon with Oscar was my calling, not simply a task to tick off from a list. It would be the making of me—of us both—and the ripples of the decision would be felt for years to come.

I couldn't wait to begin.

CHAPTER 3

I had never been to Scotland. I'd never even been out of England, only straying from the comfortable familiarity of London for the occasional seaside holiday to Ramsgate as a child. Most folk would say I wasn't suited for world travel, and they would be right. My scholarly life and introverted nature had ill-prepared me for the challenges that came with venturing to another country.

Those challenges began on the first day and only grew worse as the day wore on.

Heavy traffic delayed our arrival at King's Cross Station, but fortunately our train's departure was also delayed by an hour, so we made it with time to spare. But our late departure meant I worried about arriving in a strange city in the dark. That worry, combined with the movement of the train, made me feel a little queasy in the stomach, so I didn't eat the sandwiches I'd packed for the journey.

When I stood to alight from the train as it pulled into Edinburgh's Waverley Station, I felt dizzy from the lack of sustenance and lost my balance. I toppled into the burly, bald-headed Scotsman reading a newspaper on the seat opposite. Thankfully he didn't get cross. He merely chuckled into his red beard as he helped me to regain my balance. He commented in a strong Scottish accent about my inability to hold my drink.

"Oh, I'm not drunk," I quickly assured him.

He merely chuckled again and handed me my hat. I hadn't noticed it fall onto the seat beside him.

I hurried after Oscar and wondered how I'd ever cope with the language barrier when we eventually voyaged to the continent, since I could barely understand a fellow who spoke English. Although I spoke French reasonably well, I doubted it would help me outside of France, and my Latin and Ancient Greek wouldn't be useful at all in day-to-day conversation. It was yet another thing to worry about.

Having collected our luggage from the porter, Oscar stretched his back and rolled his shoulders. "That was a long journey, but at least I read an entire book. What about you, Gavin? You didn't seem to be concentrating very hard on your notes."

I'd planned to jot down ideas for a new book about the history of magic but had given up barely an hour into the journey. "I found concentrating difficult," I told him.

Oscar's gaze followed the big Scotsman who'd shared our cabin as he joined the queue to buy a newspaper from one of the lads near the kiosk. All of the newspaper sellers were popular, with a small crowd gathering to make their purchase. It would seem the Scots enjoyed their evening papers.

When Oscar turned back to me, an odd little smile teased his lips. "Was he the reason you couldn't concentrate?"

I pushed my glasses up my nose. "I think I simply need the comfort of my own environment."

The smile briefly flared before his lips flattened. "Let's find a cab."

I picked up my valise by the handle and trailed after Oscar, whose long strides made it difficult for someone as short as me to keep up. "There might be none left by the time we battle through this crowd."

"We'll be fine."

I refrained from asking him why he'd think that. I didn't want to annoy him on our first day together. With a hand to my hat, I glanced at the big Scotsman again. He'd purchased his paper and was reading intently, as were several other passengers. According to the front-page headline, a second local girl had disappeared from the same area as the first a mere day earlier.

I followed in Oscar's wake as he forged a path through the crowd on the platform to the exit. I'd vowed not to let my anxiety hold me back. I may have only made that vow to myself, but I planned to keep it. I wouldn't fall at the first hurdle.

Even so, I kept as close to Oscar as possible. He was quite comfortable jostling the other passengers without being rude or aggressive. He looked calm and untroubled, whereas my heart beat a little faster at every interruption, of which I encountered a few. It seemed as though newsboys shouted the latest headlines in *my* ear, not Oscar's, the messenger runners bumped only *me*, and lost tourists seemed to think I knew directions to this hotel or that.

A souvenir seller with a wooden tray tightly packed with trinkets attached to a leather strap tied around his neck stepped in front of me. "Postcard, sir? Map?" He pointed to the items in his collection, both bordered with a red tartan.

"No, thank you." I tried to move around him, but he blocked my path.

"Authentic tartan scarf? Ribbon for your sweetheart back home?"

"Excuse me." I managed to dodge around him and avoid the trolley full of luggage that a porter was pushing toward me, only to step into the path of a fast-moving empty trolley.

The porter ordered me to move aside. I bit down against the stinging pain in my lower leg from where the trolley had hit me and limped on, only to realize Oscar had disappeared.

Tightness constricted my chest, and I felt a little lightheaded again. Recognizing it for the anxiety I sometimes experienced when I was out of my depth, I was able to breathe through it as a doctor had once shown me to do. With the tightness easing, I focused on the exit ahead and followed the rest of the passengers who'd alighted from our train.

Oscar waited for me beside a carriage while a station porter secured his valise to the roof. "Apparently it's a bit chaotic at the moment because they're expanding the station. Some of the entrances and exits are closed off and one of the platforms has been demolished to make way for new ones. Nothing that we Londoners aren't used to, though." He clapped me on the shoulder and steered me to the rear of the vehicle. "Give the groom your luggage and let's get on our way."

"Groom? Isn't he a station porter?" Even as I said it, I realized the man wasn't dressed in the North British Railway porter's uniform with shiny brass buttons and NBR embroidered on the jacket lapels. The youth couldn't have been older than twenty and wore the cap and sturdy boots of an outdoor member of staff for a private household.

"Kinloch sent a carriage to collect us. Hand over your case, Gavin. We don't want to keep the fellow waiting." When I didn't move, Oscar took my valise and passed it to the groom. His gaze, however, focused on the station entrance behind me.

"But we're not supposed to meet Kinloch until tomorrow," I said. "It's getting late and I'd rather check into the hotel now."

The final rays of sunlight bathed the sandstone of the station building in golden splendor, but it was fading fast. My stomach growled, reminding me I hadn't eaten since breakfast. Hopefully we could find a decent chophouse near the hotel. I didn't fancy eating my sandwiches. The cucumber would have made them soggy after a long day stuffed in my valise.

Oscar indicated the carriage. "We can't be rude to Kinloch and ignore his invitation."

"You didn't tell me we were being collected upon our arrival. You let me think we had to find a hackney."

A commotion behind me caught Oscar's attention, followed by a booming American voice. "You there! What do you think you're playing at?"

Oscar wrenched open the carriage door. "Get in, Gavin!"

The coachman, draped in a tweed greatcoat, despite the fine weather, pinned Oscar with a sharp glare. "Ye *are* Mr. Defoe, aren't ye, sir?"

I opened my mouth to answer, but Oscar grabbed my arm. "Get in, and he can't throw us out."

"Oscar!" I cried.

A dark-skinned woman dressed in navy-and-white striped silk, matching hat and white gloves, pushed past me from behind and thrust her closed umbrella across the doorway before I could step into the cabin. "Excuse me, gentlemen, I believe you've made a mistake. This vehicle is for us."

I'd expected an American accent like the man who'd

shouted, but it was English, and an upper class one at that. The woman was extraordinarily pretty with high cheekbones and brown eyes fanned by long lashes. She was slim and tall—taller than me, but a little shorter than Oscar.

He couldn't take his gaze off her. "I believe we were here first, ma'am, but since you're also paying Mr. Kinloch a visit, we'll allow you and your companion to join us." He raised his brows in question at the coachman.

"It's all the same tae me." The coachman hunkered down into the collar of his greatcoat as he faced forward.

Oscar smiled as he held out his hand to the woman to assist her up the step.

She accepted it, returning his smile as she locked her gaze onto his. There was something quite mesmerizing about her, a quality that was more than mere physical beauty. It was her confidence, I realized, as I watched her with Oscar. She seemed so utterly sure of herself, of every lithe movement of her limbs, every languid blink of those large eyes, and every syllable that fell from her lips. I envied her that confidence.

I was so transfixed by her that I wasn't aware she'd forced Oscar to take a polite step back by drawing close to him. Nor did I notice she'd lowered her parasol until a man brushed past me and climbed into the carriage. Oscar noticed too late, too, and opened his mouth to protest.

Before he could utter a word, the woman stabbed the end of her umbrella into his left shoe at the toes. "It's not nice to take something which isn't yours."

Oscar winced in pain although he quickly plastered a

smile on his face as the woman climbed into the carriage. "If you'll give us a moment to remove our—"

The woman closed the door and the American man commanded the driver to make haste.

"Our luggage!" Oscar cried.

The groom who'd secured it to the roof had to run to catch up with the vehicle as it pulled away from the curb. He managed to jump onto the footboard at the back before it sped off.

"Damn and blast!" Oscar growled. "Why didn't you stop them, Gavin?"

"Me? Why not you? Oh, that's right, you were too busy admiring that woman's...eyes." My uncharacteristic sarcasm earned a blink of surprise from Oscar.

Then he broke into a grin. "I'm glad to see you *can* stand up for yourself."

"Sorry. I'm tired. But it was *their* transportation. You heard the coachman ask if you were Defoe." I stared in the direction the carriage had gone, but it was already out of sight. "What on earth is he doing here, and heading to Mr. Kinloch's residence, the same as us? It's such an extraordinary coincidence."

"Not really."

"What do you mean?"

"I'll explain on the way, but first, we have to make sure Defoe doesn't get the opportunity to buy that book out from under our noses."

"Not to mention retrieve our luggage. I do hope that groom managed to secure it properly."

Oscar wasn't listening. He strode to the open cart that had been waiting behind Mr. Kinloch's carriage. He spoke to the driver as two station porters wrestled a trunk onto the back, then he signaled to me to join him.

"This is Defoe's luggage. The driver has agreed to let us ride to Kinloch's place with it."

I went to climb up beside the driver, but he ordered us to the back. Oscar assisted me onto the tray and sat down, his back against a steamer trunk with the initials J.J.D. embossed in gold on the side. A second, more battered trunk of similar size was positioned behind it. It must belong to the woman. If it bore a monogram, I couldn't see it. There was other luggage, too, including a third trunk and smaller valises. Mr. John J. Defoe and his female companion did not travel light.

Oscar inspected the lock on the trunk behind him. "Magic warmth," he said, sounding impressed.

I looked for a clean place to sit but couldn't find one. If I had my luggage I could retrieve a towel from my valise and sit on that. I was considering whether I wanted to stand or sit when the decision was made for me. The cart lurched forward, causing me to fall to my knees beside Oscar.

"All right, Gavin?" he asked.

I sat down and dusted off my trousers. "I'm fine. Oscar, I don't think it's right to show up unannounced in the evening at Mr. Kinloch's house. We're not expected until tomorrow."

"Are you willing to lose the Mackenzie book to someone else over a matter of politeness?"

I twisted so that I could see the back of the driver's head. "My good fellow, could you go a little faster? Time is of the essence." At Oscar's arched brows, I added, "I've been wanting to get my hands on a copy of Mackenzie's *Laws of Witchcraft* for years."

"These old lassies dinnae know the meaning of fast," the driver said over his shoulder.

"Could you teach them the meaning for thruppence?" Oscar asked.

"I reckon they'll learn real quick for six."

Oscar grumbled about the cost as he handed him a sixpence. The driver urged the horses with a flick of the reins and a guttural order in thickly accented Scots.

The horses responded and we were soon passing slower moving vehicles. I settled back against the trunk and admired the handsome buildings of the city. Soot and grime had settled onto the balconies and roofs, but that only added to the gothic charm of the buildings in the old part of the city. I caught sight of the castle, hunkered on a hill like a crookbacked old man calmly surveying his flock.

"Magnificent," I murmured. "Did you know it's one of the most besieged places in Great Britain? Perhaps the world?"

Oscar didn't answer. He was frowning, his gaze distant. "Do you think that was Defoe's wife?"

So that's where his thoughts lay. I should have guessed. "I doubt it," I said.

"Why? Because he looked about forty, and she didn't seem older than mid-twenties? Wealthy men have much younger wives all the time, Gavin."

"Usually it's their mistresses that are much younger." I pushed my glasses up my nose to study him better, only to find he was glaring at me.

"You shouldn't assume she was his mistress," he said. "Not on such short acquaintance."

Heat warmed my face. "You're right. That was ungentlemanly of me. She may not be his mistress, but I do know she's not his wife."

"How?"

"I made inquiries after we saw his letter to Lord Coyle. I thought that if he was a collector of magical things, like Coyle, then others may have come across his name. One of the things I learned from an acquaintance was that Mrs. Defoe's name is Ava and she's aged thirty-eight."

"Impressive. I didn't think we'd need to know anything about the man, so hadn't given him another thought, but you went so far as to research him."

My cheeks warmed even more at his praise.

"What else did you learn about him?" Oscar asked. "We may need all the information at our disposal if we are to come up against him in a bidding war for the book."

A bidding war we had no hope of winning. I didn't say that to Oscar, however. He seemed in rather a good mood, despite everything, and I didn't want to deflate it.

"His father made a fortune in the railroads, and John J. inherited the controlling share of the company ten years ago. He's based in New York, and has a second house in Newport, which the family uses in the summer. Apparently, it's modeled on the Palace of Versailles, and is quite magnificent."

The cart turned right, away from the parklands and castle into the New Town with its warm honey-colored stone terraced houses and wide streets. I watched a lamplighter lift his pole to light the streetlamp outside a gentleman tailor's shop. Unlike the electric lights at the station, these ones were still gas.

"What I don't understand," I went on, "is why Defoe is here in Edinburgh at the same time as us, heading to the house of the same man. Indeed, he had an invitation and was collected by Kinloch's staff. Why didn't Kinloch afford us the same courtesy?"

"Because we're not rich," Oscar said.

"I suppose that could be the case, but why is Defoe here at all? And why now? He wrote that letter to Coyle years ago."

"And Coyle never wrote back. But his widow did, quite recently."

"You think this is Lady Coyle's doing?"

Oscar nodded. "Hope must have read Defoe's letter after our departure and sent him a telegram. He corresponded with Kinloch then immediately booked his passage to get here in a matter of weeks."

"We can't blame her," I said. "She mustn't have realized *we* wanted that particular book, or she wouldn't have contacted Defoe."

"Ha! Of course she realized. Lady Coyle is a wasp disguised as a butterfly, with a particular dislike of India. She knows we're working for India and she would like to see her lose for a change." He pointed a finger in the air to make a point. "Also, I hear her late husband's money is drying up because she's fond of both gambling and luxury. It wouldn't surprise me if she demanded a price from Defoe in return for information about the book. It would be so like her—" He cut himself off and cleared his throat.

I suspected he'd heard the vehemence in his voice and disliked it. I knew it wasn't all directed at Lady Coyle. His opinion of well-to-do ladies was colored by his experience with his former fiancée, Lady Louisa. Clearly he was still bitter. Whether he was bitter about their relationship ending, or the reason for it existing in the first place, I couldn't tell and wasn't prepared to ask.

I faced the direction we were heading as we turned into a curved street lined with elegant terraces on one side and a private garden square on the other. Oscar was right about Lady Coyle being somewhat cruel toward Matt and India. He was also right in that she desired money, otherwise why would she have married such an awful man as Lord Coyle? She wasn't alone in liking money, however. Sometimes it seemed the entire world wanted to acquire more of it. Even the centuries of persecution of magicians, and the recent tensions over new laws that ensured they weren't discriminated against, boiled down to money. The artless were afraid their businesses would fail because magician-made goods would become more desired. There were no longer riots in the streets, but even someone like me, who preferred to keep their head down, could sense the tensions still bubbling beneath the surface.

I only hoped Mr. Kinloch wasn't blinded by Mr. Defoe's money. We couldn't outbid one of the richest men in the world.

Going by the fact Mr. Kinloch had sent a carriage to fetch Mr. Defoe from the station, however, it seemed we'd already lost.

CHAPTER 4

While Oscar gave our names to the butler who greeted us, I watched the cart driver unload the luggage. He'd stopped behind the carriage that had delivered Mr. Defoe and his companion. I was surprised to see it still there, since it must have arrived several minutes ahead of us. The reason became clear when the coachman stepped down from his perch. Hands on hips, he twisted from side to side, his gaze scanning the trees and bushes of the garden beyond the fence opposite. He seemed to be looking for something. Or someone.

I peered into the semi-dark, trying to determine if any of the shadows were person shaped, when I spotted movement out of the corner of my eye. A maid emerged from the steps leading down to the neighboring house's basement service area. Her gasp reverberated around the quiet, curved street.

She stared at me, eyes wide with fear.

I smiled in what I hoped was a reassuring way, but all it did was force her back a step. The hand on the black iron railing tightened its grip.

"You've got nothing tae fear from them, Agnes." Mr. Kinloch's coachman jerked his head at Oscar and me. "They've just got off the train at Waverley, so it's not them."

Not us? What was he referring to?

Agnes's grip on the railing loosened a little, then she ran back down the steps and disappeared into the house.

I cleared my throat in an attempt to get the coachman's attention. It worked, but instead of a polite 'Aye, sir?', I received a scowl that put me back in my place. Their conversation had been a private one, and it was none of my business to intrude.

I set aside my curiosity and turned back to Oscar as Mr. Kinloch's butler invited us to wait in the entrance foyer.

The towering fellow peered down his nose at us. "I'll see if Mr. Kinloch's taking callers." I was surprised to hear he was English.

"We know Mr. Defoe is already here," Oscar said tightly.

"Oscar," I hissed.

Oscar drew in a deep breath and let it out slowly. He forced a smile for the butler. "We'll be waiting." He turned to me. "Gavin, ask the coachman to take down our luggage." He indicated the valises still strapped to the top of the carriage. "We'll leave them here in the foyer until our business is finished."

I glanced at the coachman, only to find he was still watching me. Light from the streetlamps reflected in his eyes, making him look as though he was lit from within like a supernatural creature. The shadows cast by his craggy features only added to the devilishness.

I swallowed heavily. "Perhaps *you* should ask him, Oscar."

With a shrug, he trotted back down the steps and spoke to the coachman.

The coachman said a few words in return then climbed back up to his perch. He flicked the reins, and the horses moved off. Oscar returned to me without the valises.

"Our luggage!" I cried. "Where is he taking it?"

"He's driving around to the mews. We're to collect them from the coach house when we're finished with Kinloch." Oscar ushered me back into the foyer as the butler returned.

"Mr. Kinloch will see you now," he intoned. "Follow me."

He led us up the staircase, past walls with rectangular patches on the wallpaper where paintings must have once hung for many years. Were they sent off for cleaning, or had he sold them? If the latter, it would seem Mr. Kinloch was experiencing financial trouble. That would make him quite desperate to get what he could for the rare book, making our task of purchasing it even more difficult. We could offer him a good sum, but not a large one. Unlike a railroad magnate.

The butler led us into a comfortable if rather old-fashioned reception room where an array of knickknacks were clustered on every inch of table surface like barnacles on the posts of a seaside pier. Seeing all the clocks, candlesticks, and little dog statues put to rest any notion that Mr. Kinloch was experiencing financial difficulty. Those would be the easiest and therefore the first to sell off.

A man approached and extended his hand to Oscar. "Good evening. I'm William Kinloch. Mr. Barratt, I presume?" His accent was an educated English one with the merest hint of Scottish brogue. His age was difficult to guess with the threads of gray through his beard but not his sandy-colored hair. The only lines on his face appeared at the corners of his eyes when he smiled, which he did throughout the greeting. He was impeccably dressed in a pin-striped suit, but the tie's knot was a simple one and sat slightly askew. A good valet ought to have done better. Perhaps Kinloch didn't have a dedicated one and instead had his butler or a footman perform double duties.

Mr. Kinloch shook Oscar's hand then turned to me. "And you must be Professor Nash."

I wondered how he'd managed to guess correctly. "A pleasure to meet you," I said. "We're sorry to intrude." I nodded an awkward greeting to the two familiar figures seated on the sofa.

The beautiful woman gave a slight nod in return, as if she were barely deigning to acknowledge our presence. She sat stiff-backed beside Mr. Defoe who sprawled into the corner of the sofa as if he owned it. Indeed, as if he owned the entire place. He could certainly afford to buy the house several times over, even though it was one of Edinburgh's finest, so Oscar had informed me when he'd learned of the address. Unlike the woman, Defoe smiled, but it didn't improve the equine features that the thick, black sideburns attempted to soften. Indeed, somehow it made him seem condescending, as if he were smiling because he knew he'd already beaten us to the book. He couldn't have been more than forty, younger than I expected for a wealthy magnate. Then I remembered he'd inherited his fortune, not made it.

"Thank you for receiving us like this," Oscar said to Mr. Kinloch. "We hope we're not too late to make an offer for the Mackenzie tome."

"Not at all. Mr. Defoe has made me an offer, but I've declined to entertain it until speaking to you. You were the first to contact me, after all, so it's only fair you are given the right to make the first bid. I expected to see you tomorrow, as planned, but since you are here, we can begin. Allow me to make the introductions. Mr. John J. Defoe and Miss Adele Wheeler, please meet Mr. Oscar Barratt and Professor Gavin Nash. Miss Wheeler is Mr. Defoe's assistant."

That cleared up one mystery.

Oscar hadn't taken his gaze off her since shaking her hand. "Then it must be you, Miss Wheeler, who arranged for Mr. Kinloch's coach to collect you from the station. Please forgive our attempt to borrow it."

"It wasn't me," she said, voice silky smooth.

"I offered to collect Mr. Defoe and Miss Wheeler," Mr.

Kinloch said. "Given they're new to our shores, I thought it the hospitable thing to do."

Mr. Defoe lifted a hand from the sofa arm in dismissal, the motion little more than a twitch as if he could hardly be bothered. "I trust you won't attempt to steal what's mine again, Barratt." The American drawl held a hint of steel that had my pulse leaping.

"How is your foot, Mr. Barratt?" Miss Wheeler indicated Oscar's foot that had been stabbed by the end of her parasol at the station.

He waggled it. "Fortunately these shoes are my sturdier traveling pair."

"That's good to know." The unspoken words 'for next time' hung in the air.

Oscar's eyes brightened with amusement.

Miss Wheeler looked annoyed that her comment had done as little damage to his ego as her parasol had to his foot, which only made Oscar's eyes brighten more.

Mr. Defoe reached into his inside jacket pocket and removed a cigar and gold vesta box embossed with his initials. "Mind if I smoke, Kinloch?"

"I... er..." Mr. Kinloch trailed off as Mr. Defoe plugged the cigar into his mouth and struck a match. "Not at all, if Miss Wheeler doesn't mind."

"She's used to it." Smoke billowed from Mr. Defoe's mouth along with his words.

Miss Wheeler sat as calm as could be beside him, not looking at all perturbed. Not moving a muscle either.

Mr. Kinloch signaled to his butler. "Three whiskeys,

Redmayne, and a cup of tea for Miss Wheeler. Or do you prefer sherry?"

"I prefer whiskey," she shot back. "I hear your distillery makes a very fine single malt."

Mr. Defoe's chuckle erupted from the depths of his chest as if she'd said something amusing. We all glanced at him, but he didn't share the joke with us. Miss Wheeler gave no reaction. It was as if he wasn't even there.

Redmayne glanced at his employer who nodded. The butler bowed out of the drawing room.

Mr. Kinloch asked how our journey had been. Oscar answered politely while Mr. Defoe merely grunted and puffed on his cigar. He left it to Miss Wheeler to explain that it had taken them almost two weeks to reach Scotland from New York. As the cigar smoke drifted across to her, she suddenly stood.

"Don't get up," she said as Mr. Kinloch, Oscar and I went to stand out of politeness. "I'd like to take a turn about the room. I need to stretch my legs."

"You must want to freshen up after the long journey," our host said.

"And miss the negotiations? I'll stay, but thank you for the offer."

Mr. Kinloch asked me about my work at the university. He listened while I told him I'd resigned from my position some time ago to co-write a book with Oscar, and now we planned to travel together.

"Mr. Barratt's first book created quite the stir on this

side of the world," Mr. Kinloch explained to Mr. Defoe and Miss Wheeler. "Indeed, it changed the course of history."

"I wouldn't go that far," Oscar said. "It merely explained magic to the artless. History was changed by others."

"Your letter said you're a magician."

Oscar nodded, but did not clarify that he was an ink magician. "Are you a magician, Miss Wheeler?"

She'd been standing beside a round table by the window where a newspaper was perched on the edge, but now looked up. She opened her mouth, but Mr. Defoe answered before she could speak.

"I am a magician—iron, of course."

Miss Wheeler's lips flattened, and she turned away to look out of the window.

Mr. Defoe sucked on his cigar.

Oscar wouldn't be put off. "Are you American, Miss Wheeler?"

"I'm English," she said, glancing over her shoulder at him. "But you knew that from my accent."

"You may have been brought up in England and moved," he shot back, unperturbed. "How long have you worked for Mr. Defoe?"

She crossed her arms. "Has anyone ever accused you of asking too many pointless questions?"

"Frequently, but in my defense, they're rarely pointless, it's just that no one knows it except me. In this instance, my questions are most definitely not pointless."

Miss Wheeler studied him beneath thick dark lashes as if trying to assess if he were teasing her.

Mr. Defoe withdrew his cigar from his mouth and grunted a laugh. "You're wasting your breath, Barratt. Adele has been subjected to the flirtations of more charming men than you and has ignored them all."

Rather than be put off by the caustic remark, Oscar laughed softly. "If that's considered flirting where you're from, then it's no wonder she has ignored these so-called charmers. Forgive my journalist's nosiness, Miss Wheeler. It's a habit I've found difficult to break when someone intrigues me."

Miss Wheeler suddenly turned back to the window, as something on the street caught her attention. Or perhaps she simply didn't want to risk being sucked in by Oscar's warm eyes and easy manner. He was a very good flirt. Many women had fallen for him after only a brief conversation. Indeed, sometimes he didn't have to speak at all. I'd once seen a young widow leave a soiree in his carriage after their gazes connected across the room. He was very handsome, after all, and after his relationship with Lady Louisa ended, he used his handsomeness to his advantage. He'd become quite indiscriminate of late, taking a different lover every month, or so it seemed. Not that he ever boasted about his conquests. Indeed, he was rather discreet, and most of his friends wouldn't have realized. I spent a great deal of time with him and could be quite observant when I put my mind to it.

Redmayne entered carrying a tray with a decanter and

four tumblers but did not immediately set it down. He blinked at Miss Wheeler, still staring out of the window. If it wasn't for that blink, I'd have thought he hardly took notice of any of us. He had an air of professional indifference about him. But that blink, accompanied by the hasty depositing of the tray and his striding toward her, had me wondering what had upset him.

He reached past her and snapped the thick curtains closed, then snatched up the newspaper. "Would you like me to pour, sir?"

Mr. Kinloch signaled for him to leave. The butler bowed out, newspaper clutched firmly in his hand. Miss Wheeler watched him go with a narrowed gaze.

I'd caught a glimpse of the headline before he left. As with the newspaper at the station, it was an article about the second girl to go missing in a week. But this newspaper's headline was more provocative: *Witchfinder Strikes Again.*

The subheading was less attention grabbing, but more informative: *Second Woman Magician Missing from Moray Place.*

We were currently sitting in a townhouse on Moray Place, discussing the sale of a book about the persecution of witches. The coincidence was striking.

Perhaps it wasn't a coincidence at all.

CHAPTER 5

I sipped my whiskey and suppressed the cough that rose when the liquid burned my throat. I'd never taken to the liquor, finding it too rough for my liking. I preferred wine or port but hadn't wanted to refuse our host. He looked pleased when Oscar praised it and took another sip, so I praised it, too. Mr. Defoe swallowed a mouthful then rested the tumbler on his thigh without commenting.

He was keen to get on with the purpose of his visit. "Let's begin negotiations. I'll offer double."

"Double of what?" Oscar asked. "Mr. Kinloch hasn't mentioned a price, and we haven't made an offer."

"It doesn't matter what your offer is. I'll double whatever you say."

"And if we double *your* offer?"

"You can't afford to."

"That's a little presumptuous."

"My good fellow, if you had money, Kinloch would have offered to collect *you* from the station." Mr. Defoe spread his arms wide, inviting Oscar to challenge his assessment.

Oscar sipped his whiskey.

Mr. Kinloch cleared his throat. "Gentlemen, before we discuss the financials, may I ask each of you why you're interested in the book?"

Mr. Defoe had been about to plug the cigar back into his mouth but paused. "How is that relevant?"

"It may not be, but I'd like to know nevertheless. In deference to the distance you've traveled, you may go first, Mr. Defoe."

Oscar's jaw firmed in annoyance that we'd not been afforded the courtesy. The movement was so subtle that I doubted either man noticed, and Miss Wheeler was once again peering out of the window after having re-opened the curtains. She seemed disinterested in the negotiations. I tried to signal to Oscar that going second was to our advantage, but he wasn't looking at me.

"Gracious of you, Kinloch," Mr. Defoe said. "I was thrilled when I received Lady Coyle's telegram mentioning her discovery of an old letter from you to her husband about the book. I've been trying to get my hands on a copy for years."

"Why?" Mr. Kinloch pressed.

"It's rare."

"Yet not particularly valuable, except to scholars." Mr. Kinloch indicated me with a wave of his whiskey glass.

"I'd like to study it," Mr. Defoe said. "Is that scholarly enough for you?"

"And when you've finished studying it? What will happen to it?"

"I'll add it to my bookshelves, of course."

Mr. Kinloch waited, but Mr. Defoe had finished. Our host invited Oscar to speak.

Oscar sat up straighter. "As I said in my letter, Professor Nash and I are traveling the world to collect books about magic with the aim of forming a public library. Matt and India Glass—Lord and Lady Rycroft—will be its patrons. They're spearheading magician reforms in Great Britain," he added for Mr. Defoe's benefit. "They were instrumental in ending the persecution of magicians here, the effects of which have rippled around the world. I believe the United States recently passed similar legislation."

"There you have it," Mr. Defoe declared. "Our intentions for the book are both scholarly. The only way to separate us is the amount each will offer."

"Not true," Mr. Kinloch said. "Mr. Barratt and Professor Nash will display it publicly. You'll lock it away. No one will get to study it unless *you* approve."

Mr. Defoe started to laugh, then realized Mr. Kinloch was quite serious. "Ah. I see what you're doing. You're a good negotiator, I'll grant you that. Very well, let's talk actual numbers. What do you want?"

"If it was about money, I would have sold it to Coyle years ago."

Mr. Defoe scoffed. "He didn't offer what I will." When Mr. Kinloch remained silent, Mr. Defoe swirled the whiskey in his glass, as casual as can be. "Let's not pretend you don't have a price in mind. We all know the saying about a Scotsman and his money."

Mr. Kinloch's nostrils flared at the stereotypical slight.

Mr. Defoe failed to notice and barreled on. "Let's also not pretend what this is really about. Eh, Barratt?"

"I don't know what you mean," Oscar said.

"I'm a magician, as are you. Neither of us wants the Mackenzie book for its historical or scholarly value."

I leaned forward to interrupt. "I want it for its scholarly value."

Mr. Defoe ignored me. He kept his gaze firmly on Oscar. "We both want it because it references another book about tattoo magic that makes a man fly. Getting our hands on *that* book is our true endgame."

"Why?" Mr. Kinloch asked. "How can you use the tattoo magic to your advantage?" He seemed unsurprised by the interest in that particular reference. It wasn't news to him.

"I know a spell to make iron fly and want to experiment with blending it with the tattoo ink spell," Defoe said.

"You don't know for certain if the book Mackenzie references has the actual spell in it to make a tattooed man fly."

"You're right. I won't know until I find it and read it." Mr. Defoe thrust his chin in Oscar's direction. "Do you know a flying spell, Barratt? What is your particular magic type anyway?"

Oscar merely glared back, silent. I sat unmoving, too worried to even blink in case I gave away that Oscar did indeed know a flying spell, and an ink one at that. If either man could use tattoo magic to make themselves fly, it would be Oscar, not the iron magician. But I felt in my bones it was something we didn't want Mr. Defoe to know.

Mr. Defoe huffed, giving up on waiting for Oscar to answer. "Well, Kinloch? How much?"

Mr. Kinloch stood and crossed the room. He opened the door and Redmayne entered. He must have been standing there, waiting. "Mr. Defoe and Miss Wheeler aren't staying the night, after all. Please reload their luggage onto the carriage and ask Blackburn to take them to the hotel of their choice. I can recommend the Windsor on Princes Street. I believe Mr. Barratt and Professor Nash are staying there."

Redmayne wordlessly disappeared to follow orders.

Mr. Defoe chuckled but it held an edge of uncertainty. "Interesting negotiating technique."

"This isn't a negotiation. I'm inviting you to leave."

The chuckle died on Mr. Defoe's lips. He shot to his feet and pointed the cigar wedged between two fingers at Mr. Kinloch. "I thought the British did business like gentlemen."

Miss Wheeler swept past her employer and offered her hand to Mr. Kinloch to shake. "Thank you for the whiskey. It's a smooth blend. Good evening, gentlemen," she said to

Oscar and me, albeit mostly to Oscar. "It's been interesting." She left without a backward glance, the pleats of her dress swaying with the movement of her hips.

Mr. Defoe wasn't quite ready to give up, however. He pointed the cigar in Oscar's face, his own face turning quite red. "You'll regret this, Barratt."

Oscar flicked the ash that had fallen from the cigar off his trousers. "Would you like to add 'This isn't over?' to complete the cliché?"

Mr. Defoe's face grew even redder and the muscles in his jaw bunched as he worked himself up to respond.

Before he could, the butler returned. Upon Mr. Kinloch's nod, he stepped up to Mr. Defoe. Redmayne towered over the smaller, slimmer man. "The carriage is almost ready. Please follow me." I'd not noticed how intimidating Redmayne was until that moment. He was a tall, solid fellow with large hands. He could easily win a fight against the American. Unless Defoe used a spell to fling iron objects at us, that is.

I kept one eye on the fire irons.

Mr. Defoe strode to the door only to point the cigar once more, this time at Mr. Kinloch. "Fool. I could have made you rich."

"You're the fool for thinking I want to be rich. I am quite comfortable, thank you." Mr. Kinloch exchanged a glance with his butler who came up behind Mr. Defoe.

The American tugged on his cuffs and marched out of the room, Redmayne dogging his steps.

Oscar strode to the window and looked down at the

street below. I could just make out his smile in the reflection. The smile suddenly vanished, however, and he leaned even closer to the glass.

I joined him at the window. "Is something the matter?"

"Miss Wheeler appears to be arguing with Defoe."

"About the book? His obnoxious behavior?"

"I can't tell. She gestured toward the neighbor's house then back at this one."

I followed his gaze to where Mr. Kinloch's carriage waited. Miss Wheeler blocked the carriage doorway with her parasol, as she had done at the station to us. She said something to her employer that made him bristle. His response seemed to appease her, and she lowered her parasol. I couldn't make out her expression in the weak light cast by the streetlamps. She climbed into the carriage ahead of Mr. Defoe.

I expected the coachman, Blackburn, to drive off, but he suddenly glanced up at us. Oscar and I quickly stepped back, out of sight from below.

"Professor Nash, Mr. Barratt, are you ready to see it?" Mr. Kinloch opened a drawer of the small desk in the corner and removed a book a little bigger than his hand.

My pulse quickened. "Is that it?"

He indicated I should sit on the sofa, then brought the book over. "*A Treatise on the Laws of Witchcraft and Maleficium in Scotland* by His Majesty's Lord Advocate George Mackenzie," Mr. Kinloch said as he handed the volume to me. "Calfskin binding, rather plain with some blind tooling decorations in the outer corners. It's in remarkably good condition."

"It is," I said on a breath as I opened it. I resisted the urge to sniff the old paper. The one time I'd done that in front of Oscar, he'd looked at me as if I were mad. Instead, I carefully turned the page.

"Mackenzie was a remarkable man," Mr. Kinloch said. "Complex too, by modern standards. As Lord Advocate, he defended the use of torture to secure confessions, yet he believed so-called witches were ordinary elderly women. His thoughts on witchcraft went against those of his contemporaries. That's why one particular incident he recounts in this book is of utmost importance to the study of the history of magic, as we now know it. He once met a woman whom he believed was a real witch. In another famous work penned by Mackenzie, he describes how he studied and questioned her, without torture, and learned that she could manipulate wood using spells."

Oscar approached and stood behind us to peer over our shoulders at the book in my lap. The mention of magic and a wood magician, rather than witches and witchcraft, had drawn his attention.

Mr. Kinloch continued. "Mackenzie investigated her and discovered that her family knew an ancient spell to work wood into beautiful and sturdy objects. He seems to have learned their spell, although it's not clear how he got wind of it. He tried to recreate the woodworking effect using the same words of the spell but couldn't. We know now that he failed because he wasn't a wood magician, but at the time he didn't know about magic being an inherited trait. He was artless and magic was kept secret, for obvious reasons."

"Remarkable," I said, reading the lines of Mackenzie's story myself. "It redefines what we know of the history of magic discovery by the artless. I don't know of any other eye-witness accounts about magic written by an artless that aren't colored by prejudice and religious zealotry."

Oscar clapped me on the shoulder. "India will find this fascinating. I can't wait to show it to her, and Matt too, of course. Kinloch, at the risk of sounding like Defoe, what are you asking for it?"

"I think ten pounds is a fair price. It may sound like a lot, but it *is* rare."

Ten! I could buy a wardrobe full of clothes for that. Oscar, with his finer tastes, could probably fill half a wardrobe, however.

"Five," Oscar countered.

Mr. Kinloch considered the offer. "If it was about the money, I would have given Defoe a chance to bid. I want the book to go to a good home, but I do need to get a reasonable price for it." His gaze flicked around the room, taking in the bare floor and the sparse furnishings. "Meet me at eight, Barratt?"

Oscar held out his hand. "Seven, and you have a deal."

"All right. Seven pounds it is."

They retreated to the desk to make the financial exchange, while I scanned more pages. Most of the text was quite mundane and bogged down by the language and legal terminology of the seventeenth century. But one name caught my eye. Indeed, it appeared quite a lot.

"Are you related to the Kinloch mentioned here?" I asked when they rejoined me at the sofa.

Mr. Kinloch's eyes narrowed with his slight wince. "He was my ancestor. I hope that knowledge doesn't color your opinion of me."

"Not at all. The sins of Thomas Kinloch are not your sins."

"Who was Thomas Kinloch?" Oscar asked.

I handed him the book and pointed at some lines near the top. "He brought several women to trial. They were convicted of witchcraft and burned at the stake, which was the punishment at that time in Scotland, as opposed to England where convicted witches were hanged."

"Think of him as Scotland's equivalent to Matthew Hopkins," Mr. Kinloch said.

"The Witchfinder General?" Oscar asked.

I nodded as I accepted the book back from him. "This is a strange thing for your family to keep, considering Sir George Mackenzie doesn't write favorably about your ancestor."

"Indeed he doesn't," Mr. Kinloch said. "Thomas Kinloch deserves to be painted as the villain he was. I agree that it is a rather strange thing to pass down through the generations. I'm not really sure why it has been. It was kept under lock and key ever since I can remember. As one of the few surviving copies—perhaps the only copy—I presumed it was to keep it safe from thieves. But when I read the pages about Thomas Kinloch, I wondered if it was to keep the awful truth about my family's history from the world." He shrugged. "It no longer matters. As you say, my ancestor's actions don't reflect on me, centuries later." He tapped the book's cover with his finger. "It's a valuable resource now, and I believe it should be studied by scholars like yourself, Professor. We live in a new age of enlightenment for magicians, and with enlightenment comes education and understanding. Books like this one need to be available to all, not just a few rich men like Defoe, or the late Lord Coyle."

"We quite agree," Oscar said. "Thank you for accepting our offer. Matt and India will be thrilled."

"I must admit, if it wasn't for them, I wouldn't be selling at all."

I peered at him through my spectacles. "Why not?"

"I've long wanted this book to be made available beyond these walls. It was simply a matter of who should get it. Lady Rycroft is a powerful magician, but also a cautious and sensible one. She doesn't use her magic to benefit herself, unlike Defoe, who turned out to be as greedy as a I feared." At my arched brows, he added, "He wanted to find the book referenced in this one that contains a tattoo magic spell. I doubt he, an iron magician, could make a tattooed human fly, but I wouldn't put it past him to find an ink magician who could." His sharp gaze suddenly pierced Oscar. "According to the biography in your book, *you* are an ink magician and may have that ability. Be careful, Mr. Barratt."

"I won't use tattoo magic for my own benefit," Oscar assured him. "Merely for my own amusement."

"So I presumed, thanks to your association with Lord and Lady Rycroft, which is why you now have that book in your possession. But that's not what I meant. I meant be careful of Defoe, and people like him. When he discovers your magical craft is ink, and gets his hand on that flying tattoo spell, he may use you."

Oscar's smile was as bright as the sun. "Thank you for your concern, but I'll be fine."

They shook hands, and Mr. Kinloch called for the butler to show us out. Redmayne, however, had disappeared.

A commotion downstairs had us all turning to the door. A man's loud voice could clearly be heard demanding to be released.

Mr. Kinloch frowned. "What the devil?" He strode out of the drawing room.

Oscar followed with me close behind, the book in hand. We trotted down the stairs to the entrance hall where Redmayne had a man's arm twisted behind his back. The fellow's hat had fallen off and lay upended on the tiles, and his unruly curls spilled over his forehead.

"Unhand me!" he cried. "Let me go or I'll have you arrested for assault!"

"Redmayne?" Mr. Kinloch asked. "What's going on?"

"Are you Kinloch?" the man asked before the butler could answer. "Tell your thug to release me!"

Redmayne tightened his grip, causing his captive to

hiss in pain. "He came in via the service entrance, sir. He upset the female staff with his accusations."

Mr. Kinloch's spine stiffened. His nostrils flared. "Get out!"

I jumped at his shout. Confrontation always made me want to run away. If I could become invisible, I would. Instead, I melted into the shadows, the book clutched to my chest.

At the same moment, Oscar stepped forward, as if my retreat directly caused his advance. "What accusations has this man made, Kinloch?"

Mr. Kinloch shook his head ever so slightly, as if it were too stiff to move more. "It doesn't matter."

The interloper, however, seemed pleased to be able to enlighten him. "He abducted those magician women."

CHAPTER 6

M r. Kinloch scrubbed a hand over his face. It shook. When it came away, he looked older, more haggard, and less like a refined gentleman.

Oscar moved up beside him, a calm act of solidarity. Whether Mr. Kinloch appreciated it, I couldn't be sure from where I stood, a little back from the scene. *I* appreciated it, however. Oscar's self-assured capability was a balm to my frayed nerves.

Oscar addressed the intruder. "You can't just accuse someone like that. What evidence are you basing it on?"

"I wrote about my theory in this evening's—"

"*You* wrote that!" Mr. Kinloch cried. "You scoundrel. I'll sue you and the publication for defamation."

The journalist lifted his chin in defiance. "You weren't named."

"The implication will be enough for some to identify me." Mr. Kinloch wrenched open the front door. "Throw him out, Redmayne." As the butler muscled the journalist forward, Kinloch added, "If you return, I'll have you arrested."

The journalist put a booted foot to the doorframe to resist Redmayne's efforts. "History repeating itself—the Kinlochs arresting folk they dislike."

Was he referring to Thomas Kinloch, the Scottish version of the Witchfinder General? Good lord. His accusations and article weren't based on evidence. They were a witch hunt based on an ancient family connection.

With a sneer, he lowered his foot and succumbed to Redmayne's efforts to manhandle him down the front steps to the street where the butler released him. Redmayne shoved him for good measure.

Mr. Kinloch tossed the man's hat after him. "You're a disgrace to your profession."

The journalist swiped up his hat and shook it at our host. "Where are they, Kinloch? Where are the women?"

The neighbor's front door opened and two men emerged. The one wearing a smoking jacket must be the master, while I suspected the other was his butler or footman. I assumed they'd assist Redmayne to remove the journalist from the area altogether, but both seemed more intent on watching Mr. Kinloch with rather nasty expressions.

Mr. Kinloch pretended he hadn't seen them, but I was quite sure he had. A flicker of relief cast over his face upon the return of his carriage, driven by Blackburn. It was driving so fast that the journalist had to quickly step back onto the pavement or risk being hit.

Mr. Kinloch cleared his throat. "Good evening, gentlemen. My coachman will take you to your hotel. I do apologize for this business."

"Good evening," Oscar said.

I was about to repeat the farewell, but Mr. Kinloch disappeared inside before I could.

The butler escorted us down the steps and opened the coach door. "Blackburn will retrieve your luggage from the mews before taking you to the hotel. It's not far."

I glanced along the street to see where the journalist had got to, but he'd disappeared.

Oscar addressed the butler. "Who were the two abducted women?"

"I have to return inside, sir."

"Were they housemaids? Residents? How old were they? Where were they when they were taken?"

The coachman turned on his perch to glare at us. "Get in," he growled.

I hurriedly climbed into the cabin.

Oscar peered up at Blackburn. "You must be out and about on this street a lot. Have you noticed anything untoward? Anyone who shouldn't be here?"

Blackburn barked an order at the horses, and the coach lurched forward.

Oscar had to jump into the carriage as it rolled away. He pulled the door closed and sat alongside me. "Bloody hell. That was suspicious behavior. Forget Kinloch. My money's on Redmayne or Blackburn. Perhaps they're both in it together."

"Oscar! You can't say that, even in jest. They were merely reacting to the tense situation. They'll be worried about the trouble that article stirs up." We turned a corner so fast that I slid into Oscar who found himself crushed up against the side. Fortunately, it was well padded in green velvet so if he hit his head, it wouldn't hurt.

He assisted me back to my side. "Still got the book, I see."

I looked down at the volume in my hand. I held it so tightly my fingers ached. "Oh, yes. I'm not putting this beauty at risk."

When we turned another corner at an equally frenetic pace, Oscar banged his fist on the roof before gripping the leather hand strap. "Steady on, Blackburn! We want to arrive in one piece."

His words had no effect, and we spent the rest of our journey trying not to collide with one another.

Later, after finally eating some cold leftovers the hotel kitchen staff sent up, I lay in bed and read through the Mackenzie book. Oscar had gone to bed in the room next to mine. I ought to be tired after such a long day, but found I couldn't sleep. The book was far too interesting.

Finally I found the reference to the real magician Sir George Mackenzie had discovered. He called her a witch, but from the description, it was clear she was a carpenter magician. I climbed out of bed and pulled on my trousers and a shirt. I tucked it in, sort of, and drew up the suspender straps, then picked up the book.

I stepped out of my room and tiptoed to Oscar's door. I lightly knocked. If he was awake, he'd hear it. If he was asleep, I'd keep my findings until the morning. I hoped he was awake, however.

The door opened, and it was clear from his attire that he hadn't yet gone to bed. Not that he was dressed. Not completely. He wore no shirt, just an undervest tucked into his trousers. He had a more muscular physique than I expected for a man whose former occupation required him to sit at a desk for a large part of his day. Much more.

He crossed his arms over his chest, making the muscles bulge. He leaned a shoulder against the doorframe. "Everything all right, Gavin?"

"Everything's fine. I wanted to show you something in the book."

"You found the reference to the other book that mentions tattoo magic?"

"No." His face fell. "I found the reference to the real magician Mackenzie encountered." I glanced past him to see an array of newspapers spread across the bed. "You've been doing some late-night reading yourself."

He dragged his hand through his hair, ruffling the locks. He looked tired. I probably did, too. "Come in," he said, stepping aside.

I brushed past him and inspected the newspapers. I picked up the one I'd seen Redmayne remove from the drawing room, the one with the provocative headline. "Those poor women. I hope they find them."

"That's the article written by the journalist we met at Kinloch's." Oscar stood behind me and peered over my shoulder. "He doesn't name Kinloch, but he points out that the abductions occurred very close to the house where the descendant of Scotland's most notorious witchfinder general lived."

"There was no such occupation. It was a self-appointed title, or perhaps one given to Thomas Kinloch by the public." I was being pedantic, but I felt strongly that journalists ought to strive for accuracy.

"Sensationalism sells." Oscar sat on the bed against the pillows, his long legs stretched out in front of him. He picked up one of the other newspapers. "That masthead is very popular, so the night porter told me when he gave me these copies."

"So poor Mr. Kinloch will soon have an angry mob brandishing pitchforks on his doorstep."

"When the public work it out, he will."

We both knew they would, sooner or later.

I sat on the bed, too, and rested a hand on his shin. "This is none of our business, Oscar."

His gaze fell to my hand. I quickly withdrew it. "I know."

"And yet you want to investigate."

"Do I?" he said idly.

"You have that look in your eye."

He pressed his finger and thumb into his eyelids, as if that could erase the feverishness. "What look?"

"The same one that appeared when you first heard about tattoo magic." I brandished the book. "You won't rest until you get what you want, and in this case, what you want is to find those girls."

"Women, not girls. The first to be taken was a nineteen-year-old maid who worked in the house next to Kinloch. She took some scraps out for the horses late yesterday and never returned. The bucket was found in the mews beside one of her shoes, an effigy made of straw propped up against it. The second was the twenty-two-year-old niece of the owner of the house next to that one, two doors from Kinloch. She was visiting from Aberdeen and went out for an early walk this morning in the garden opposite. A cry was heard by a passing coachman, but when he went to check, there was no sign of anyone, just a 'small doll made of straw dressed like a lady.' Those are the exact words of the witness." Oscar picked up one of the other papers and handed it to me. "The witness's name was Blackburn."

"Kinloch's coachman?" I took the newspaper and read. "I wonder what else he saw or heard. Hopefully the Edinburgh police are thorough and learned all they could from him."

"As a witness or suspect?"

I gasped. It was shocking to think we may have ridden in a carriage driven by an abductor, but the more I thought about it, the more I agreed that Blackburn must be considered a suspect. He could come and go from Moray Place *and* the mews behind the townhouses without raising suspicion.

I lowered the newspaper and regarded Oscar, surrounded by more newspapers on the bedspread. His hair fell over his forehead as he read, and he lightly tugged on his lower lip. He was completely absorbed. I didn't think it was healthy for him to take such an interest in the abductions, particularly since we were leaving Edinburgh the day after next. Now that we had the book, we could have left in the morning, but we had tickets for the train for the following day, so had decided to spend our spare time sightseeing instead.

It was beginning to look like the only sights we would see would be Moray Place and the mews running behind it.

Oscar glanced up, his intense gaze connecting with mine. I couldn't look away, even if I wanted to. "You're watching me."

"No, I'm not."

"It's all right, Gavin."

"I wasn't watching you."

His lips curved up at the corners. "Then why are you blushing?"

"It's hot in here."

"Is it? I hadn't noticed."

"That's because you've taken your shirt off." I tugged on my collar. It felt too tight all of a sudden. I considered removing my shirt, too, but decided against it. It was an action that could be misconstrued.

Oscar set the newspaper down beside him. "Gavin—"

"We could contact Willie's husband, D.I. Brockwell, and ask him to offer his assistance. He's an excellent detective."

"Gavin—"

"Brockwell and Scotland Yard can advise the Edinburgh police by telegram. I'm sure it will help. That way, we don't need to get involved."

Oscar sank back into the pillows with a sigh. "Brockwell's advice will be invaluable, I agree. I'll send a telegram in the morning."

"And we'll leave the following day, as planned?"

He gave me a flat smile, the sort someone gave when they wanted to placate. "We have the train tickets for an early departure."

I knew him well enough to know that I wouldn't get a direct answer, no matter how many times I asked. Oscar wasn't prepared to commit to leaving while there was a mystery to solve.

I admired him for his strong sense of justice. I truly did. It was a rare quality, and it set him apart from most people. Indeed, it raised him above them. But I worried where that desire for justice would lead him, and what lengths he would go to see it served.

It turned out that I had cause to worry.

* * *

The following morning, I awoke to a sense of foreboding, but it wasn't until I finished shaving at the washstand and went to put on my shirt that I realized why.

The book was missing.

After leaving Oscar's room, I'd returned to mine and stayed up a little longer to read more. I was so tired, however, that I'd read for a mere fifteen minutes before going to bed. I'd not locked the book away in my valise but left it on the table beside the valet stand where my clothes hung. The table was now empty.

Oscar must have come in and taken it. But how had he got into my room without a key?

I checked the door, only to find that it was indeed locked. I tried the window. It opened easily. I leaned on the windowsill and looked over Princes Street, already bustling with carriages, carts, and pedestrians below. Well below. My room was on the fourth floor. No one could have scaled the external wall and got in. Whoever took the book had entered via the door. It *must* have been Oscar, having got a key from one of the staff because he didn't want to wake me.

I quickly threw on my shirt and tied my tie. I slipped on my shoes and went to open the door when there was a knock from the other side.

"Gavin? Are you awake?"

I wrenched the door open. "Oscar, do you have the book?"

"No, you have it. How tired were you last night when you left?"

"I don't have it." I indicated the table. "I left it there. You didn't come in and take it while I was asleep?"

His face drained of color. "No."

I pressed my fingers into my temples where a headache was starting to bloom.

Oscar pushed past me. "What's that?" He picked up something from under the table. "Gavin." The ominous tone clanged a warning and set my heart thudding in my chest.

"Yes?"

"Was this here when you went to bed?" He held up a small effigy made of straw and wearing a pair of spectacle frames fashioned from thin wire.

My stomach dropped. My mouth went dry.

"It must have fallen off the table," Oscar said.

"What does it mean? Am I the next person to be abducted?"

"I don't know, but it is a message."

"Message?" I said weakly. My brain was having difficulty grasping his meaning. Usually sharp, it was failing me badly.

"A message that says the abduction of those women is linked to last night's theft of the Mackenzie book. I don't know who would want those women or why, but I do know one person who desperately wanted the book."

So did I—John J. Defoe.

CHAPTER 7

Oscar would have charged off to confront Mr. Defoe then and there if I hadn't blocked the doorway. The fire in his eyes raged so fiercely that I worried he'd forcibly move me out of the way.

I put up my hands, prepared to press them against his chest if I had to. "Oscar, don't do anything rash."

"I won't," he growled.

"We can't accuse him of abduction and theft."

"You're right. We need to gather evidence first."

"We can't even accuse him then. If we find evidence pointing to him, we take it to the police. They can handle it."

"*We* can handle it."

"You're forgetting something, Oscar." At his blank look, I continued. "He's an iron magician. He can tear sharp slivers off iron things and fling them at us with the movement spell. We'll become human pincushions!"

"Defoe may have lied about knowing the iron-moving spell. Iron magicians are incredibly rare, and we only know of one who knows the spell to move iron. If he could do that spell, India and Matt would have heard of Defoe and warned us, but they didn't. Your grandfather was an iron magician, wasn't he? Could he make it fly?"

"No, and I understand that not every magician knows a movement spell. My point is that Defoe says he can, so we must assume he told the truth until we learn otherwise. It's too great a risk to confront him. I say we take our suspicions to the police. We'll warn them about his magic."

Oscar lowered his head, his shoulders slumping. When he looked up again, he was more composed, his brow cleared of the furrow that had formed there upon first mentioning Defoe.

"All right," he conceded. "We'll go to the police and offer our assistance."

I collected a clean handkerchief from my valise and plucked my hat off the valet stand. I followed him out of the room and locked the door, pocketing the key just as my stomach growled.

"We'll go after breakfast," he added.

There was no point protesting. I was hopeless in the mornings until I'd eaten a good breakfast and downed it with a cup of coffee. I quickened my pace to keep up with Oscar's long strides as he headed for the stairs.

"India once said it was a good idea for you to accompany me on these book collecting jaunts," he said. "Perhaps this is why. I tend to act without thinking, whereas you…"

"Tend to think without acting?" I offered. It was hardly a flattering assessment of my overly cautious nature, but it was an accurate one.

"I think she meant you and I complement one another. Separately, our strengths are fine, but not special. But together, we make a formidable team." He clasped my shoulder. "We're going to find those women, Gavin, and get the book back from Defoe *if* we work together."

"With the police." I peered up at him and nodded. Considering the nature of what we'd set out to do, he was in quite a good mood.

"You need new spectacles," he said. "Ones that fit better."

"Pardon?"

"Those keep slipping down your nose."

"Do they?"

"You've never noticed you're constantly pushing them back up?"

I touched the bridge of my glasses only to self-consciously lower my hand. "No, I've never noticed."

He wasn't listening, however. He'd spotted two people on the landing below and increased his pace. "Defoe!"

Oh, lord. I suspected my influence wasn't going to stop him doing something rash now.

Mr. Defoe smirked. "I told you." He spoke to Miss Wheeler, standing beside him.

She eyed Oscar's rapid descent toward them, her gloved hand tightening its hold on the umbrella she held.

"Want to sell it already, Barratt?" Mr. Defoe asked. "I'm afraid my offer will not be the same as—"

"Don't play games, Defoe. Where is it? Where's the book?"

Mr. Defoe laughed, only to stop when no one joined in. "What do you mean? Have you lost it?"

"We haven't *lost* it. You stole it."

Mr. Defoe's eyes widened. "My God, you *have* lost it! How could you have misplaced it mere hours after getting it?"

Oscar's fists closed at his sides. "Hand it back and we'll forget this happened. Otherwise..."

"What? You'll punch me? And here I thought you a gentleman, Barratt."

"I'll notify the police," Oscar growled.

Defoe snorted.

Oscar stepped toward him. I lunged to stop him, but was too late. The point of Miss Wheeler's umbrella pressed into his stomach. Oscar could have pushed it aside, but he seemed too taken aback by the unexpected move to do anything other than stare at her, mouth ajar.

Defoe snorted again. "Take my advice, Barratt, don't cross Adele. With or without an umbrella, she's formidable when she wants to be."

Oscar put up his hands in surrender. "I wasn't going to hit him," he said to Miss Wheeler. "I just want to search him for the book."

Defoe opened his jacket to reveal he had nothing in his inside pockets or tucked into his waistcoat. "Adele, open my valise. Our trunks have already been taken down by the porter, but you can search those too, if you like, Barratt."

With a final glare for Oscar, Miss Wheeler lowered her umbrella and opened the valise Mr. Defoe had set down upon our approach. Inside was a traveling writing desk inlaid with mother-of-pearl, which she also opened, and papers. The Mackenzie book wasn't among them.

"We don't have it," Mr. Defoe reiterated when his assistant closed the valise. "If you've lost it—"

"It was stolen," Oscar snapped. "Gavin left it on a table in his room, but it was gone when he woke up this morning. Aside from us, you are the only other person who knew we had it and also wanted it."

"You can't be certain of that. Perhaps Kinloch informed someone. Perhaps Kinloch himself stole it back."

"Why would he do that?" I asked.

"To have both the money *and* the book."

"He struck me as an honorable man."

Mr. Defoe had answered me without looking at me, but now he managed to tear his attention away from Oscar. From the anger vibrating off him, I rather wished I'd stayed silent. "May I offer you some free advice, Professor? You shouldn't trust a man on such a short acquaintance. It gives him the upper hand."

His words were friendly on the surface, but the underlying tone rippled with anger. He now turned that anger onto Oscar.

"That book is valuable, Barratt. I've not found another and I've been searching for years."

"We know that," Oscar said through gritted teeth. "We also know you only wanted it for the reference to tattoo magic. Hence our conclusion that you are the one who likely stole it last night."

Mr. Defoe pointed his finger in Oscar's face. "You two should never have been given custodianship of such a valuable item. A journalist and an academic," he spat. "I'd wager neither of you have ever wielded anything more dangerous than a pencil. You can't protect yourselves, let alone an object in your possession."

Oscar lunged, but Miss Wheeler was quick. She whacked his shin with her umbrella.

"Ow!" He hopped on one leg and rubbed his shin. "Was that necessary?"

Miss Wheeler stepped closer to Oscar while Mr. Defoe stepped back, content to let her take charge of the situation. It was most peculiar. While I'd seen Willie use physical violence, I'd always thought her rather unique among women. She dressed like a man, behaved like a man, and was raised by outlaws in America's Wild West. Miss Wheeler, with her educated English accent, expensive clothes and pristine white gloves, was definitely not like Willie. Yet she made me feel rather vulnerable. I suspected she could beat me soundly with nothing but her umbrella.

Oscar didn't seem quite so vulnerable, although he looked bewildered as he took her in anew.

"You're rather easily riled, aren't you, Mr. Barratt?" she asked, voice warm and velvety like a fine mulled wine.

"Defoe can say what he likes about me," he shot back. "But not my friend."

"You called him a thief. Did you expect him to let that slide?"

Oscar lifted his chin, not willing to retract his accusation.

I, however, had considerable doubts that we were right. Mr. Defoe seemed worried about the disappearance of the book. It could be an act, but if so he was a good actor. I was about to point out a fact that Oscar had missed, but Miss Wheeler did it first.

"Think about it, Mr. Barratt. Would we still be here if we stole the book? No. We would have left on the first train out of Edinburgh."

"Someone stole that book, Miss Wheeler. It didn't walk out on its own."

"Then let's work together and find out who took it, shall we?"

"We'll report the theft to the police," I told her. "There's no need for your help with that."

Neither she nor Oscar was listening to me. They didn't even look at me.

"Why do you want to help us find it?" Oscar asked her. "We won't be selling it to you once its safely back in our possession."

"Because knowing who has it is better than not knowing. You said yourself, the book is going to form part of a library collection in London that will be open to the public. We are the public. Or will certain people be barred?"

"Of course not," Oscar assured her. He glanced at me. "Do we trust them, Gavin?" By asking me, it meant he wanted to give in. I wondered if that had anything to do with the remarkable woman with the wine-dark voice and lovely brown eyes, who was rather handy with an umbrella.

"There's no need for anyone's help," I said again. "We're only going to the police station to report the theft. We don't need anyone to accompany us."

"We'll go there soon," Oscar told me. "We should find out what we can from the staff here first, then take that information to the police." At my hesitation, he added, "We may as well be of use, and we are already here. Time is of the essence, Gavin."

He made a good point. Finding the book was secondary to finding the two women taken from Moray Place. With the effigy linking the theft to their abductions, we were now involved, whether we wanted to be or not. We might as well be of use and, as Oscar implied, the wheels of Edinburgh's constabulary may grind as slowly as those in London.

I agreed to question the hotel staff but, first, I needed something from Mr. Defoe. "If you and Miss Wheeler wish to help, then it would be appreciated. Four heads are better than two. But I need your assurance that once the book is found, you won't try to take it from us."

"You have it," he said. "You bought it, Professor. It's yours."

I couldn't bring myself to fully trust him, but accepted his word. We might need some of his financial support to fund the search if the police were unhelpful. Money had a way of loosening tongues. After we got the book back, Oscar and I would need to be extra vigilant in keeping it out of Mr. Defoe's clutches.

"Shall we begin?" I asked him.

"Not me. I was going to read some papers on the train, but I might as well do it in my room. Adele will assist you."

He looked amused, while Miss Wheeler watched Oscar carefully, almost defiantly, as if daring him to scoff or protest that a woman could be of use.

She didn't know Oscar like I did. I wasn't surprised when he asked her if she was ready to begin immediately. "I'm sure Mr. Defoe can carry his own valise back to his room," Oscar finished.

Mr. Defoe picked up the valise then moved closer to Miss Wheeler. He whispered something in her ear then brushed past me and headed up the stairs.

I cleared my throat as I gathered the courage to finally utter a retort I'd thought of earlier in our exchange. "I'd like to point out that pencils *can* be very dangerous, in the right hands." This time, I felt self-conscious as I pushed my glasses up my nose. I felt even more self-conscious when

Mr. Defoe laughed without slowing his pace. I wished he hadn't glanced over his shoulder and seen me blush.

"Why do you work for that man?" Oscar asked Miss Wheeler.

"Why do you ask such impertinent questions?" She set off down the stairs. "I was in need of employment, and Defoe offered me a position as his assistant. Given the color of my skin and my background, few men would. Probably none. Whatever you think of him, he has always treated me well."

"Your background?"

"Is none of your business."

Oscar smiled.

We reached the hotel foyer where Oscar made inquiries about extending our stay before asking the clerk if he'd seen anyone go up the stairs who wasn't a guest. He had not, but nor had he worked overnight. We spoke to the manager, housekeeper, porters and doormen, but no one suspicious had been seen around the hotel. The night porter had finished his shift but was still there, and he also denied seeing any strangers entering the hotel.

We had to go to the police empty-handed, after all. Oscar seemed more frustrated than me as he strode across the foyer and pushed open the door himself before the doorman could reach it. He waited on the pavement while I asked the doorman for directions to the police headquarters. It wasn't far, so we walked.

"I think we should question Kinloch and his staff," Oscar said.

Miss Wheeler stamped the end of her umbrella into the uneven pavement with each step, using it as a walking stick. "So you do think he stole it back despite what you said to Defoe?"

"There's something we haven't told you. Something that links the theft of the book to the abduction of two women from Moray Place."

Miss Wheeler's eyes widened. "What is it?"

"We'll tell you on the way."

"To the police station," I said sternly.

Oscar kept an eye on Miss Wheeler's umbrella as it firmly struck the pavement. "Since we're going to work together, may we call you Adele?"

"No."

He wasn't put off. Indeed, he seemed to delight in her prickliness. "You may call me Oscar if you like."

"I don't like. Remaining formal is best, given our brief acquaintance."

"It may be brief, but it has been intense up until now, with the likelihood of it becoming even more so by the time this endeavor is finished."

One gloved finger tapped on the umbrella handle. "How is your shin, Mr. Barratt?"

"Bruised, but—"

I jabbed him in the ribs with my elbow. Miss Wheeler's eyes flared briefly, with amusement, if I wasn't mistaken.

Oscar rubbed his side. "I was going to say that I deserved the bruise. I acted rashly and coarsely. I apologize unequivocally, Miss Wheeler. Hopefully you won't see that side of me again."

One corner of her mouth ticked up before flattening again. "What did you want to tell me on the way? Why do you think the theft is linked to the abductions?"

Oscar removed the straw effigy from where he'd tucked it into his inside jacket pocket. "We found this in Gavin's room. Straw effigies were left behind at the scenes of the abductions, and now this. It suggests a link. I can't think why the two incidents are connected, only that they must be."

"They *appear* to be," she pointed out. "You shouldn't assume without more evidence."

Oscar tucked the effigy back into his pocket. "A third effigy placed at the scene of the crime is not enough for you?"

Miss Wheeler simply lifted one shoulder in a half-hearted shrug. Even that movement was elegantly understated. To think we were dragging this lady into an investigation involving the abduction of women. It was foolhardy and unthinking, not to mention ungentlemanly.

"I've changed my mind," I said. "You shouldn't help us, Miss Wheeler. We'll return you to the hotel after we speak to the police. Perhaps we all should step down and simply let them handle it."

"No," both Oscar and Miss Wheeler said.

"But Miss Wheeler is a woman!"

"Thank you for noticing, Professor."

I bit the inside of my cheek. "That's not what I meant. I

mean, yes, I did notice you were a woman. How could I not with..." My gaze fell to her not-insignificant chest before I realized how inappropriate that was, so I raised it to her face again, only to see her eyes dancing merrily. My face flamed.

Good lord, what was wrong with me?

I appealed to Oscar. With his smoother tongue and confidence in all situations, especially around women, I thought he could explain better than me.

He chuckled. "We'll take good care of Miss Wheeler, Gavin. As for continuing to investigate or not, I strongly suggest we do. We have connections to Scotland Yard through Brockwell, and an understanding of magicians like no other. We are also tenacious and intelligent. The police need us more than we need them."

"My my, you are arrogant," Miss Wheeler said.

"Very well," I said before Oscar could retort. "We'll offer to conduct our own investigation. But not with Miss Wheeler. We shouldn't have dragged her into it."

"You didn't," she said. "I volunteered."

"She wants to find those women just as much as we do," Oscar said. "Perhaps more."

"Do I?" she asked idly.

"I noticed your interest at Kinloch's. You surreptitiously read the newspaper then peered out of the window, as if searching for something or someone. Or were you keeping an eye on the street and garden square opposite?"

"I was simply bored with the negotiations."

Oscar didn't continue, thankfully. He knew when to

back off. As a journalist, he often had to speak to sources or witnesses, and he was very good at getting them to reveal more than they wanted about themselves. Sometimes that meant *not* asking questions, and merely allowing a silence to stretch thin enough that his source wanted to fill it.

Miss Wheeler didn't fill it, however.

Oscar did something quite uncharacteristic for him. He filled the silence himself. "Where did you grow up, Miss Wheeler? You said yourself your accent is English, but there are many different English accents. I can't determine which county you're from."

Miss Wheeler tapped her finger on the umbrella handle again. "Is he always this nosy, Professor?"

I grinned. "He doesn't like mysteries."

"Then he is doomed to a life of frustration. The world is full of mysteries, I've found. Some will never be solved, certainly not in our lifetime. Unless Mr. Barratt is prepared to make peace with that, he will drive himself mad trying to find answers when none can be found."

Oscar sniffed. "First of all, you can both stop talking about me as if I'm not here. Secondly, I am prepared to let some mysteries remain unanswered. For instance, the question of why such a beautiful and intelligent woman works for such an unpleasant man like Defoe is one I've accepted I may never know the answer to. But the question of why that woman didn't hesitate to step out with two men she has just met intrigues me greatly. I would very much like to find the answer to that one."

She'd held his gaze as he spoke—or perhaps he held hers—but she now released it by looking away and staring into the distance. "I suspect that is a mystery you *will* solve, Mr. Barratt."

He smiled. "I look forward to it."

She didn't respond and remained silent for the remainder of the brisk walk.

CHAPTER 8

The Edinburgh police were keen for any information that could lead them to the two abducted women. The detective in charge of the case invited us to report in front of several colleagues in the police chambers. Oscar told them about the theft and showed them the effigy.

It did not go well. The policemen returned to their desks, grumbling about their time being wasted. One even accused us of making the effigy ourselves.

"We're telling the truth," Oscar said heatedly. "Why would we try to trick you?"

"People do," Detective Inspector Smith said.

Oscar huffed a frustrated breath. "We should work together. Do you have a telephone? Contact Scotland Yard and speak to D.I. Brockwell. He'll vouch for us."

I expected a flat refusal, but the detective obliged. He disappeared to make the call, and returned several minutes later to advise us that Brockwell had indeed suggested that we could help. "While ye have my permission tae find out what ye can from witnesses, I'm not convinced your thief and the abductor are the same person."

"Why not?" Oscar asked.

D.I. Smith opened the top drawer of his desk and removed two straw effigies of women. He set them down on the table, and asked Oscar to place our effigy alongside them. When he did, it became clear they were different. The two from the abduction sites were twice the size of ours, and the color of the straw was different. The straw they were made from was lighter, as if it had been exposed to the elements longer. The general shapes were different too, with ours having limbs that were proportionally too short for the body.

"Now ye see why the men are skeptical of your motives?" D.I. Smith returned the two effigies to his desk drawer. "It's no' unusual for crimes that appear in the newspapers to be copied by the public."

"Why?" I asked.

The detective shrugged. "People are strange, sir."

Miss Wheeler picked up our effigy and studied it. "We would still like to definitively rule out a link between the theft and abductions. What can you tell us about the women who were taken?"

D.I. Smith hesitated before folding his hands on the desk. Without referring to his notes, he told us everything he knew in his rhythmic Scottish accent. It amounted to little more than what we'd read in the newspapers. The first woman to be abducted was Mary, a housemaid of Mr. Kinloch's next-door neighbor. She'd started working there a mere week earlier. The cotton magician was an excellent seamstress, which was why she'd gained employment in the well-to-do household of a prominent judge. Mary had been abducted from the mews behind the row of townhouses. There were no witnesses, despite it being early evening. For that reason, the police assumed the abductor was someone who wouldn't be out of place in the mews. The vicinity was searched, but there was no sign of her.

The abduction of Juliette was somewhat different. It happened in the early hours of yesterday morning in the private garden square across from her uncle and aunt's house on Moray Place. The garden was for the exclusive use of the residents, who all had a key to the gate. Juliette never returned from her walk. One of the maids saw her enter via the garden gate, and it was she who raised the alarm when Juliette didn't return. A search was conducted and neighbors questioned, but only one witness came forward—Mr. Kinloch's coachman, Blackburn, who thought he heard a woman's cry coming from the garden shortly after dawn. Unfortunately, the search was poorly organized and no one could remember if the garden gate was locked or not. If unlocked, then anyone could have got in. Otherwise, it had to have been someone with access to a key, because carrying out a struggling woman would have been difficult enough without also maneuvering her over a fence or locked gate.

That was an important point, but even more interesting was the fact that Juliette had recently discovered her magical abilities. When the laws changed and magicians emerged from hiding, Juliette's mother revealed she was descended from a line of wool magicians. She was artless, but when Juliette tried the family spell, it worked. Four months later, Juliette came to Edinburgh from Aberdeen to visit her uncle and aunt, and disappeared a mere two days later.

D.I. Smith finally unclasped his hands and sat back. "The only thing connecting them is the location—Moray Place—and the fact both are magicians."

"They are also both women," Miss Wheeler added. "Did either have a particular gentleman friend?"

"None that we are aware of. If Juliette did, then he would be back in Aberdeen."

"Not necessarily."

"Are ye suggesting her suitor followed her here, then abducted her? Why?"

"Perhaps she rejected him. Do you know the reason she came to Edinburgh?"

"A holiday?" He sat forward again. "Miss Wheeler, a well-brought-up young lady doesnae meet her beau in the garden before the household is awake. She meets him in the drawing room with a chaperone present."

Miss Wheeler laughed without humor. "You may be an excellent detective, sir, but I know young women. Sometimes they arrange to meet their beaus in secret gardens, no matter how well they were brought up."

"It'll be a line of questioning for us to follow," Oscar said quickly. He stood and extended his hand to the detective. "Please let us know if you find anything further, and we will keep you informed as well."

"This is unconventional. We are no' sitting idly daein' nothing. My men have experience with abduction cases."

"Of course, but it can't hurt to have more hands on deck, so to speak. We appreciate your faith in us."

D.I. Smith walked with us out of the busy area crammed with filing cabinets and desks. Policemen acknowledged him with a nod, some greeting him by name. He hardly seemed to hear them, however. Before we reached the front reception counter, he stopped. "I hesitate tae mention this, but I think I ought. Juliette's uncle and aunt tried bribing me tae keep the whole thing quiet. They dinnae want the press to find out one of the victims was their niece."

"That's understandable," Oscar said. "The press can be relentless once they find an angle to their story, and being the niece of a prominent couple is quite an enticing angle."

"Juliette's mam came down from Aberdeen as soon as she heard and is fair upset." The detective shook his finger at Oscar. "Dinnae speak to her and upset her more."

"Speaking of the press," Oscar added, "are you going to warn the newspaper that accused Kinloch of the abductions to leave him alone?"

"They can print what they like. I cannae legally stop them."

"You can if their accusation inflames the public, who in

turn cause a disturbance, or worse, harm Kinloch." When the detective continued walking without responding, Oscar dogged his steps. "At least remind the editor that his journalists need evidence and a convincing motive. Blaming Kinloch based on a long-dead ancestor's zealotry is not enough."

D.I. Smith reached the front counter where members of the public came to report crimes, or to collect friends or family members held overnight in the cells for minor offences. "Ye havenae seen this morning's news, have ye?"

Oscar, Miss Wheeler and I exchanged looks and shook our heads.

D.I. Smith picked up a newspaper from the counter. "Seems they found a better reason tae accuse Kinloch. One I can agree is a solid motive."

I quickly scanned the article. By the time I reached the end, I could see the detective's point. The journalist suggested that Kinloch wanted to get rid of the two women because he owned a wool mill that had been turning a good profit until magicians set up rival businesses. His mill had been experimenting with blends of wool and cotton to produce softer, lighter textiles. The experiments had cost him a great deal over many years, with his creditors promised a substantial return when he found the right blend.

But no one could have foreseen the reemergence of magicians peddling their luxury goods. Cotton and wool magicians joined forces and within weeks had created a blend that was far superior to Kinloch's efforts.

"I thought he made whiskey," I said.

"That's just a wee project on the side," D.I. Smith said. "The mill has been in his family for generations. Now it's worthless."

"Are the two missing women related to his business rivals?" Miss Wheeler asked.

"No, but the journalist speculates that Kinloch is not right in the head and took the lassies tae punish all cotton and wool magicians."

"And what do you think?"

"I think I need more evidence. If ye find some, let me ken straight away."

A thin, worn-out woman bumped me as she clipped a youth over the head with the back of her hand then ordered him to get home where his Da would deal with him. While her loud admonishing caught the attention of the others waiting and many of the policeman, it was the man standing at the counter that interested me.

I tapped Oscar's arm. "That's Kinloch's butler, Redmayne."

Oscar followed my gaze. "What's he doing here?"

"Shall we ask him?"

Miss Wheeler didn't wait for Oscar's answer. She strode up to Redmayne as he turned away from the counter after speaking to the sergeant on duty. Behind me, D.I. Smith muttered something about meddling women before joining her.

"Good morning, Redmayne," Miss Wheeler said cheerfully. "Do you remember me from last evening?"

The butler was surprised to see her, but quickly schooled his features, so that by the time we greeted him, he'd resumed an imperiously indifferent expression. "Indeed, I do."

"Is there a problem at Mr. Kinloch's house?" she asked.

"Nothing for you to concern yourself with, Miss Wheeler."

"You can concern *me* with it," D.I. Smith said.

It wasn't the butler who answered, however. It was the sergeant behind the counter. "Mr. Redmayne here says a police presence is needed outside the Kinloch house, sir. The public and press are in the way and frightening the residents. Shall I send some men, sir?"

D.I. Smith nodded and the sergeant spoke to the constable seated at the desk behind him. The latter picked up his helmet, collected a colleague, and headed out of the station with both.

Redmayne thanked D.I. Smith, then asked him a rather curious question. "Has Blackburn been in to speak to you this morning?"

"No. Why would he? Has he remembered something relevant?"

"The opposite. He wants to retract his statement about hearing a cry on the morning of the second abduction. He is no longer sure what he heard. It could have been a bird."

The detective heaved a sigh. "Tell him to come and see me. I want to hear it from him."

Redmayne headed out of the building. Without a word exchanged between the three of us, we also followed.

Finding Redmayne alone was a golden opportunity none of us wanted to waste.

Redmayne had other ideas. He increased his pace. His long strides took him well ahead of Miss Wheeler and me, but not Oscar who kept apace.

"Is Mr. Kinloch all right?" he began.

"Fine, thank you, sir."

"Good, good. He must be unnerved by all this attention, as I'm sure all of the staff are."

Miss Wheeler made a face. "I thought Mr. Barratt was a journalist."

"He was," I said, my tone defensive.

"Did he write about sports? Or perhaps he wrote the social page?"

I bristled. "He was a very good journalist and wrote on all manner of topics. He is simply being polite to numb the source into trusting him."

"Numb him into boredom, you mean?" She forged ahead, closing the gap. "Mr. Redmayne, you were there when the two women were abducted."

Oscar shot her a glare. She ignored him and focused on the butler.

"I was in the house, if that's what you mean, Miss Wheeler."

"Has there been a suspicious stranger in the street or mews lately?" she pressed.

"The abductor."

Oscar tossed her a smug look.

She continued to ignore him. "Anyone you actually saw?"

"If I had seen someone, I would have reported it to the police."

"Do you know if either of the women had an admirer?"

"I do not. If I did, I would have mentioned it to the detective. His questions were very thorough."

We weren't going to learn anything by asking the same questions as D.I. Smith. If Redmayne saw anything, he would have reported it. If he was hiding something, he would keep it from us, just as he had kept it from the police.

Instead, I tried a question I didn't think the detective would have asked, because it focused on opinion rather than fact. "Why do *you* think a straw effigy was left at each scene?"

Redmayne's pace slowed. A crease formed across his brow as he considered his answer. "To incriminate Mr. Kinloch, which it has done."

"So you believe the abductor knew Kinloch was a descendant of the infamous witchfinder and decided to use that to distract everyone."

"Precisely."

"Do you think the women were taken because they're magicians?"

Redmayne's pace quickened again. "I don't know."

Miss Wheeler lifted her skirt with her free hand and hurried after him. "Or were they taken because they are female magicians?"

"I have no opinion on a motive," Redmayne snapped. "Since I do not know who took them, I can't possibly suggest a reason why. And before you ask, I do not believe it was Mr. Kinloch. Aside from the fact I know he was in bed at the time of Miss Juliette Buchanan's abduction, he is a good man. An excellent man, in fact. He does not judge harshly or too quickly, he doesn't listen to gossip, and never evaluates a person before meeting them."

That last part was oddly specific and quite unrelated to the disappearances. Why did he feel the need to mention it?

"We heard his mill is failing," Oscar said. "Apparently, it's doing poorly thanks to cotton and wool magicians, the same magical disciplines as the missing women."

"The mill is not failing, Mr. Barratt. I suggest you don't listen to nasty gossip."

"Then why has Kinloch sold off the paintings that once hung in the house?"

Redmayne suddenly stopped and rounded on Oscar. His nostrils flared and a muscle in his cheek twitched. He was trying to control his temper. If I were Oscar, I'd have stepped back, worried that one of those large fists would strike me. But Oscar merely waited, quite at ease. "He hasn't sold anything, sir. Those paintings were sent to London for appraisal."

I didn't believe him, but I kept my mouth shut.

Oscar did not. "Wouldn't it be easier to pay for an appraiser to come here? Indeed, I'm surprised there isn't one in Edinburgh." When Redmayne set off again, Oscar fell into step alongside him. "How does one even pack up a number of large and valuable paintings?"

"There is a freight company that specializes in packing them and organizing for them to be transported by rail. It all happened a month ago." Redmayne stopped outside a tailor shop. "I have to go in here. Goodbye." He pushed open the door, and slammed it shut behind him.

Oscar shrugged. "I'd finished my questions anyway. It seems they loosened his tongue a little."

Miss Wheeler barked a laugh. "*Your* questions? I'd say it was Professor Nash's question that loosened Redmayne's tongue."

"Not much, though," I chimed in.

Miss Wheeler opened her umbrella over her head as it began to lightly rain. "Professor, would you care to join me under here?"

"That's very kind of you." I offered her my arm as I slipped under the shelter with her.

"What about me?" Oscar asked.

"Didn't you come prepared for the rain?" she said. "This is Scotland, you know."

He scowled and flipped up his collar. He cast another look through the window at Redmayne chatting to the tailor before we headed off. "What do you think of his unprompted opinion of Kinloch's character? Important or not?"

Oscar and Miss Wheeler discussed the butler's responses on the way to Moray Place, but I wasn't really listening. I couldn't set aside the notion that something was amiss. We'd set out on this investigation thinking the abductions were related to the theft of the Mackenzie book, but now it seemed as though there was no link after all. The effigy that had been left in my hotel room didn't resemble the ones left at the scenes of the crime.

Should we even continue with our own investigation into the abductions if it was nothing to do with us?

I watched Oscar and Miss Wheeler out of the corner of my eye, as they discussed theories. They showed no sign of even considering backing away from the investigation now. With two against one, I didn't bother to suggest it. Besides, I wanted to find the missing women. If it meant our distraction allowed the book thief to escape the city, so be it.

What I didn't consider until later was that someone had left us that effigy for a reason, either to taunt us or lure us into a trap.

CHAPTER 9

I'd become used to seeing angry mobs protesting outside government buildings and the factories and workshops owned by magicians, but seeing one on the steps of a townhouse in a genteel street like Moray Place was far more disconcerting. Shouting accusations at a man's home, where he and his household should feel safe, was deeply personal. I wondered how Mr. Kinloch fared. Was he rigid with fear that they'd take it upon themselves to break down the door and storm inside? I certainly would be.

I spotted the journalist who'd written the article connecting him to the witchfinder of centuries past. He stood to one side of the small but vocal crowd, madly scribbling on a notepad. A photographer stood alongside him, fiddling with the lens of a camera on a tripod, a bag opened at his feet.

We decided to head directly to the mews. We had no need to speak to Mr. Kinloch. Yet.

We passed the house where the first victim, Mary, had worked as a maid. All was quiet. The curtains were closed, which was unusual for a household that employed servants whose duty it was to open them of a morning. Perhaps not so unusual, considering the to-do on their neighbor's doorstep.

The house next to that one didn't have the same air of abandonment. A man and woman watched us from a first-floor window. They stepped back in unison when they realized I'd seen them. It was the house where Juliette had been staying when she was abducted from the garden square opposite, so perhaps they were her aunt and uncle.

More police arrived as we rounded the corner, whistles blaring. We did not see the outcome of their efforts. The whistles and shouts could still be heard from the mews, but were comfortingly distant. Aside from the tapping of a hammer against a horse's shoe, the lane was relatively quiet. We found Blackburn polishing the carriage door while the groom mucked out the adjoining stables that belonged to Mr. Kinloch.

Blackburn took one look at us and returned to his polishing. "Kinloch's inside."

"We want to speak to you about the morning Juliette was abducted," Oscar said.

Blackburn paused, heaved a sigh, and continued with slow circular motions of his polishing cloth on the already gleaming carriage door.

"You were driving past the garden square when you heard a woman cry out in the early morning. Do you know the time?"

"I ain't sure of what I heard. Could have been a woman crying out. Could have been a bird. As to the time, all I can say it was around dawn. I dinna carry a fancy watch." Blackburn flipped the cloth onto his shoulder and picked up the tin of polish. "The abductions ain't your affair, sir. Go back to London and leave us to solve our own problems."

"Why are you unsure about what you heard now?" Oscar pressed. "According to the police, you were quite certain on the day of the abduction that the cry had come from a woman. Why do you want to retract your statement?"

"I told ye," Blackburn growled. "I cannae be sure."

Oscar huffed in frustration.

Miss Wheeler turned her back to Blackburn. Her voice low, she said, "This is a waste of time. He won't budge."

Perhaps we wouldn't get an answer out of the coachman about the cry he may or may not have heard, but I had a different question for him. It was a question that had rattled around in my head ever since hearing that the two abducted women were magicians.

I cleared my throat. "Last night I overheard you tell the maid from the house next to Mr. Kinloch's that she doesn't have anything to fear. You said it with conviction. Why were you certain she had nothing to fear?"

Blackburn must have known the abductor only

abducted cotton and wool magicians, and that the maid wasn't a magician, hence she was safe. It was the only explanation for why he'd not been worried for her safety.

Or so I thought.

Blackburn's eyes narrowed as he glared at me. "Because the lass is ugly."

The groom proved he'd been listening to our conversation when he suddenly stopped raking and looked up.

"Beauty is in the eye of the beholder," Oscar bit off.

"Suit yaeself." Blackburn pushed past Oscar, slamming his shoulder into Oscar's as he went.

Oscar pressed his lips together and glared at the coachman's broad back.

Miss Wheeler lifted her skirts a few inches to avoid the muck and followed the coachman. "It's not just pretty girls who are abducted, you know. Crimes against women of all description occur in every country around the world. Appearances are irrelevant." When he didn't respond, she added, "I'm sure you know that, which begs the question, why did you mention the maid's looks at all? Is it because you know the real reason those women were taken and the maid doesn't fit the bill?"

Blackburn suddenly spun around, eyes blazing with fury, fists closed at his sides. "Are ye accusing me of taking them?"

"No, she isn't," I quickly said as Oscar wedged himself into the gap between Blackburn and Miss Wheeler. He shot a fierce glare of his own back at the coachman.

Miss Wheeler stepped out from behind Oscar. "Yes, I

am. Did you take them, Mr. Blackburn? Or do you know who did?"

The fire in the coachman's eyes dimmed then extinguished altogether. He scrubbed a hand through his beard as he glanced toward the groom, who'd returned to his duties. "It wasnae me, and I dinnae ken who took the women." He glanced at the groom again and lowered his voice further. "You should look at Redmayne. He was a footman in another house years ago where a lass went missing. She was found dead days later. Redmayne came under suspicion, but was never charged. If he was innocent, why did he leave there and come tae work here?"

"How do you know this?" Oscar asked.

"I just do."

"Did you ever see Redmayne interact with either of the missing women?"

"Nae." Blackburn thrust a finger smudged with black polish into the air between himself and Oscar. "Dinnae tell anyone what I said."

"We'll have to inform the police if it becomes relevant to this investigation."

Blackburn seemed satisfied with that and began to walk off. I wasn't finished, however.

"If it was Redmayne," I said quietly so that the groom couldn't hear, "why do you think he'd leave straw effigies at the scenes of the abductions?"

Blackburn gave it serious thought before answering. "Tae throw suspicion onto Kinloch, descendant of the witchfinder. Since the lasses were magicians, an effigy puts it in folk's minds that witchcraft's a motive."

It was the same explanation Redmayne had given us earlier.

"Magic is not witchcraft," Oscar pointed out.

Blackburn turned away and strode to the coach house exit. He waited there for us to file past him.

"We should check out his story about Redmayne," Oscar said once we were out of earshot of Blackburn. "Even if it happened years ago, it's a coincidence we shouldn't ignore."

I agreed, as did Miss Wheeler, albeit with a reservation. "Blackburn offered up the information quite readily."

"We'd accused him of being the abductor," Oscar pointed out. "He had to tell us to throw suspicion off himself and onto another."

"Precisely. He may have made it up so that we'd look elsewhere for a suspect. I'm not suggesting we don't look into Redmayne's previous employment—we should—just that Blackburn didn't require much prompting, and it's something we should bear in mind."

"He also said 'were.'" At their blank looks, I added, "He said 'the girls *were* magicians.' Does that mean he knows they're dead?" I suppressed a shiver as the thought chilled me. Those poor women.

Oscar came to a stop at the stables of Kinloch's next-door neighbor, near where the first abduction took place. He indicated the horse peering over the lower stall door at us. "Would an indoor servant need to bring out the slops? I'd say it's the groom's task to feed the horses."

A spotty youth's face peered over the stall door. "I'd leave if I were you. The coachman dinnae like ink scribblers."

"We're investigators not journalists," Oscar said, approaching. "We're working with the police. Can we ask you some questions about Mary, the maid who worked here?"

"Aye. Anything tae help find her."

"Where were you when Mary was abducted?"

"In my room, above the stables, eating dinner with the coachman. We dinnae hear anything until Agnes came and asked if we'd seen her."

"Why was Mary bringing out the leftovers for the horse? Is it a task she always undertook?"

"Aye. It was an excuse tae come out here and see the horses. She liked 'em."

"Did she come out here to meet someone?" Miss Wheeler asked.

"Who?"

"A young man, perhaps. Someone she'd been stepping out with."

The groom's gaze looked past us, making us all turn. The maid who Blackburn had called ugly stood there. While her masculine features stopped her from being conventionally pretty, she wasn't awful to look at by any stretch of the imagination.

I smiled at her. "Good morning. I'm Gavin Nash, and

this is Miss Wheeler and Oscar Barratt. What's your name?"

"Agnes."

"You work in the same house as Mary, don't you?" I indicated the back of Mr. Kinloch's next-door neighbor's house.

She nodded.

"Do you know if she has a paramour?"

Agnes's gaze flicked to the groom and back. "She has a lot of 'em. She's a hoore."

I stared at her, not quite sure how to proceed after the rather nasty accusation. I'd felt sympathy for Agnes until that moment.

The groom chided Agnes for speaking ill of Mary. "Mary's a flirt," he clarified for our benefit. "The lads like her. She's bonnie."

"Did she flirt with anyone in particular?" Miss Wheeler asked.

The groom shrugged. Agnes didn't answer. I got the feeling she knew something, but wasn't sure whether to tell us.

"Did she receive letters from anyone?" Miss Wheeler prompted.

Neither servant answered.

I was wondering how we could speak to Agnes alone when Oscar asked another question. "Did everyone know she was a cotton magician?"

"Aye," the groom said.

"She wouldnae shut up about it," Agnes added. "She

was going tae leave here and use her magic tae make something of herself. She was always blathering about starting a business when she had enough money tae get going."

The coachman suddenly appeared and barked an order to the groom. "Get back tae work. You, too, Agnes. Dinnae talk tae these folk about poor Mary unless the housekeeper says."

The groom disappeared into the depths of the horse stall.

Agnes turned away, muttering. "Ain't nothing poor aboot Mary the hoore." She headed to the gate leading to the courtyard behind the house where she worked.

"She's holding something back," Miss Wheeler said, echoing my thoughts. She skipped over a puddle in the mews lane and asked Agnes to wait before entering the courtyard. "Mary had a special lad, didn't she?"

"I dinnae ken, but she did get letters from someone. We share a room, and I'd see her reading 'em in bed when she thought I was asleep."

"Did you happen to read them without her knowledge?"

Agnes didn't blink at the impertinent question. Apparently reading someone's private correspondence wasn't as shocking to her as it was to me. "Nae. I cannae read. I only know they're from a laddie because of her smile. All smug and simpering, it were." How a smile could be both smug and simpering was a mystery to me.

"Do you know what she did with the letters?" Oscar asked.

Agnes shrugged. "If she hid 'em, they're hid well. The police searched our room and said they dinnae find anything useful."

"May we conduct a search?" Miss Wheeler asked.

Agnes glanced at the rear door to the house. "Mrs. Cooper'll no' like it."

"Is Mrs. Cooper the housekeeper?" At Agnes's nod, Miss Wheeler removed a coin purse from her skirt pocket. She took out sixpence and pressed it into the girl's hand. "Will this convince you to distract her and the other staff while we look through your room?"

Agnes's eyes widened at the sight of the silver coin before she tucked it into her apron pocket. "When ye hear a loud dunt, go through this door, take the stairs tae the top. Our room's second door on the left."

Agnes disappeared inside. Moments later there was an awful clatter as a heavy pot hit the flagstone floor. A woman bellowed all manner of abusive names at the girl.

"I don't think I paid her enough," Miss Wheeler muttered as we entered the house.

We hurried as fast as we could up the steep, narrow staircase used by the servants and entered the maids' bedchamber. It was small, the sloped ceiling following the roofline of the building. I wasn't tall; even I couldn't stand erect on one side.

The three of us wordlessly searched the room, but quickly concluded there was nothing to be found in all the usual hiding places—under the mattress, inside coat pockets, under loose floorboards. We didn't dare knock on walls to locate hollowed out spaces for fear of being overheard downstairs, so Oscar and I pressed on panels instead while Miss Wheeler searched through the chest of drawers the two maids must have shared.

"I think there's a false bottom in this drawer," she said. Oscar and I joined her as she removed the folded petticoats and lifted out the flat panel of the lowest drawer. "Huzzah!" She brandished a bundle of letters tied together with a piece of cotton twine and beamed a rather dazzling smile at Oscar.

He beamed back. "Good instincts to look there, Miss Wheeler. You're a better detective than most I've met."

"If only I were allowed to be a detective."

"Their loss." His smile softened.

She quickly looked away and tried to untie the elaborate knot. "Mary must have used her magic on this. It's tight." She handed the bundle to me without bothering to remove her gloves and try again.

It wasn't easy but I managed to loosen the knot and remove the twine. I gave a letter to both Oscar and Miss Wheeler and kept one for myself. We sat on one of the beds and read. The front of each envelope simply stated 'Mary' with the address of the house. There was no return address. We compared handwriting, and it was apparent all were written by the same person. According to the name at the bottom of each letter, that person was Jack. Just Jack, no surname.

"Mine's a love letter," Oscar said as he read. "Jack says he has admired Mary for her beauty and spirit ever since she arrived at the house. He says he doesn't want to tell her his last name because he isn't ready to reveal himself to her. He writes that expressing his 'raw and powerful feelings' for her wouldn't be possible without the comfort afforded by anonymity. The rest of it lists his reasons for finding her so attractive. The language is rather flowery, but I can see why a young woman would fall for it. The letter is undated."

"This one is also undated," Miss Wheeler said. "It seems to follow on from yours, Mr. Barratt. Jack says he is ready to reveal his identity to Mary, because he can no longer simply gaze upon her from afar without her knowing who he is. The rest talks about his desire for her, that she's always in his thoughts, that he cannot eat or sleep because he's so overcome by love for her."

The letter in my hands seemed to be the third and final one in the chain of correspondence. "Jack tells Mary that he is excited to finally meet her," I read, "and that he cannot wait for the moment their eyes connect. I presume he means their gazes, as eyes cannot connect. It's anatomically impossible. Anyway, Jack tells Mary to wait for him that very evening in the mews. He'll be waiting near the rear courtyard of her residence. He stresses that she mustn't tell a soul. It is to be their special secret." I folded the letter and ran my thumb and finger along the crease. "Poor Mary was lured outside by her kidnapper." I held up the letter. "Jack."

Oscar gathered all three letters and tied the twine around them again. "I wonder if Juliette received letters from an admirer too."

"I'd bet an entire year of my wages that she did," Miss Wheeler said, standing. She watched Oscar tuck the bundle of letters into his inside pocket. "We can't give those to the police yet. We need to compare the handwriting on them to any similar correspondence Juliette received, if she did receive any."

Oscar patted the pocket. "Agreed. Now all we need to do is find out if there's anyone in the area called Jack."

"Unless Jack is entirely made up," I pointed out.

"Even if it's not, Jack is a common name," Miss Wheeler said. "It will be impossible to narrow down the list of suspects based on these letters alone."

We crept downstairs and out of the house the same way we'd entered. We found Agnes in the rear courtyard, hanging out washing. Oscar and I gave her a nod of thanks, but Miss Wheeler stopped to speak to her.

"How long have you worked here?" she asked the maid.

"Three years," Agnes said.

"Does anyone named Jack work here?"

Agnes shook her head. "The police checked, and everyone's accounted for at the time Mary went missing. It isnae one of us."

"Do you know of anyone from the area named Jack?" Miss Wheeler asked. "Someone you and Mary would have seen regularly, or would have seen you, but she wouldn't have met yet?"

Agnes looked confused by the question. "There's Jack the butcher's lad, but she's met him. He makes deliveries twice a week. One of the footmen at number eight is called Jack, but we dinnae see him much."

"Are either of them handsome?"

Agnes started to laugh, but when she saw that we were all quite serious, she sobered. "Aye, the footman is fair braw."

We thanked her and headed off. Oscar opened the gate to the mews lane.

"What about Johns?" Agnes called after us.

"Johns?" Miss Wheeler echoed.

"Men named John, who're called Jack by some."

"Do you know of one?"

"Aye. I heard our butler call Mr. Redmayne, the butler next door, John once."

Redmayne—not only did he live and work in the area and therefore could watch both Mary and Juliette, he also worked for a man whose livelihood was threatened by cotton and wool magicians. And if Blackburn could be believed, the butler had left his previous employment after coming under suspicion for kidnap.

Oscar, Miss Wheeler and I exchanged glances. Our next course of action was crystal clear.

CHAPTER 10

The police had moved the press and angry mob on from the front of Mr. Kinloch's house, but a few had found their way to the rear mews entrance. We'd planned on approaching Redmayne that way to avoid interacting with Mr. Kinloch, but decided it was better to knock on the front door now. As hoped, Redmayne answered.

He looked annoyed to see us, but did not attempt to shut the door in our faces. "Mr. Kinloch is not available."

"We don't want to speak to him," Oscar said. "We want to ask you about your previous employment."

Redmayne tried to close the door, but Oscar muscled into the gap, forcing the butler back. We followed and I shut the door behind us.

Redmayne drew himself up to his full, impressive height. He towered over me, and I would have been intimidated if I were alone with him. "This is outrageous! I'll send for the police."

"We have D.I. Smith's approval to investigate," Oscar said. "Now, about your previous place of employment. Why did you leave?"

"I was ready to be promoted from footman to butler, but that position was already taken there." Redmayne jutted his square chin forward. "There is nothing suspicious about changing employment."

"It is a little bit when it's at the same time a girl living there was kidnapped and later found dead."

"That had nothing to do with me and any suggestion that I was involved is slanderous. Now get out!" He grabbed hold of Oscar's arm, but Oscar wrenched free.

Miss Wheeler jabbed the end of her umbrella against the butler's stomach, forcing him to take a step back. "Let's keep this civilized." She lowered her umbrella. "You realize we can simply go to that house and learn more about you. This way, you have the opportunity to give your version of events."

He stared wide-eyed at her and his lips parted, but he failed to utter a word. I quite understood his shock. Miss Wheeler was a revelation.

Footsteps on the staircase signaled the arrival of Mr. Kinloch. "What the devil? Barratt, Professor? And Miss Wheeler, too. What is this all about?"

"We're investigating the disappearance of the two women from Moray Place," Oscar said.

"Why?"

"We felt compelled to assist the police." Oscar indicated Redmayne. "We learned that your butler worked as a footman at another house before coming here, and that a young woman went missing from there. She was later found dead."

Mr. Kinloch tensed but showed no surprise. "That was years ago. It also had nothing to do with Redmayne. His departure from that household to come here was merely a—" He cut himself off and his gaze slid to the butler.

"Merely a what?" Oscar prompted.

"A coincidence." Mr. Kinloch stepped around us and opened the front door. "I'm asking you politely to leave us alone."

"You've thought of something." Oscar spoke to Mr. Kinloch, but kept his gaze on the rigid figure of the butler.

Mr. Kinloch grunted. "I wondered if I would regret selling the book to a former journalist, but I'd thought you were a level above the gutter press, Barratt."

His vehemence took me by surprise. Perhaps *he* stole the book back, after all. But, if so, why leave an effigy behind? "How much do you regret selling us the book?" I blurted out.

"What?"

Oscar ushered me outside. "Not now, Gavin."

I stopped on the porch and peered past him to the doorway where Mr. Kinloch stood, arms crossed over his chest. "But—"

"Not now," Miss Wheeler repeated. She led the way down the steps.

Oscar indicated I should follow.

My nerves jumped as the door slammed shut behind us. "Do you think he's guilty? Redmayne?"

Oscar peered over his shoulder at the house. "I don't know, but Kinloch remembered something about Redmayne's previous employment. Something that I suspect is relevant."

"Surely he'd mention it to us if it were. Lives are at stake!"

"You have more faith in people than I do, Gavin." He fell into step alongside Miss Wheeler. He sported a curious look on his face, one that I couldn't quite decipher. I'd seen him flirt with women before—women he wanted to get to know more intimately—but this was something else. "I'm glad to see I'm not the only one you like to stab with your umbrella."

"Only the deserving, Mr. Barratt. Only the deserving."

"That was well done with Agnes. You got her talking."

"You could have, if you'd played your cards right."

"How so?"

"If the way she looked at you was any indication, she would have answered any questions you had. Didn't you notice the blush and fluttering eyelashes in your direction?"

"No," I said before Oscar replied.

Both turned to me, causing *me* to blush. I muttered an apology for interrupting. "Please continue your conversation as if I'm not here."

Miss Wheeler dropped back and hooked her arm

through mine. "It's I who should apologize to you, Professor, for not including you. It was rude of me."

"Oh, no, not at all. I don't want to get in the way."

"You're not in the way. Indeed, there is nothing to get in the way of. I was merely pointing out that Agnes couldn't take her gaze off your friend. You may not have noticed, but I think he did. Next time, he ought to take advantage of a suspect's infatuation with him. It could help him get what he wants."

I pushed my glasses up my nose, only to realize I was doing it and quickly lowered my hand. "Oscar is too much of a gentleman to do that."

Oscar trotted up the front steps of the house two doors down from Mr. Kinloch, where Juliette had been staying at the time of her abduction from the garden square. He explained to the butler who answered his knock that we were assisting the police with the investigation. Moments later, we were shown into the drawing room where the same man and woman who'd watched us from the window earlier now invited us to sit on their sofa.

They introduced themselves as Mr. and Mrs. Gordon, Juliette's aunt and uncle. Aged in their forties, there was nothing particularly striking about them. There was also nothing striking about the room in which we found ourselves. The house was situated in one of the best streets in Edinburgh, but a visitor wouldn't have known it from the plain and functional furnishings. There were no photographs and only two paintings hanging on the walls —one of a blue-robed Jesus praying to a golden sun, and another of a country manor house situated on the shores of a picturesque lake. Perhaps the most striking thing about the room was that none of the furniture seemed to match. The woods were different types, and the sofa was a pale green whereas the armchairs were upholstered in yellow and blue.

"We believe Juliette's mother is also staying here," Miss Wheeler said, her voice gentle with sympathy. "May we speak to her, too?"

Mrs. Gordon glanced at her husband before saying, "She's terribly upset. We don't want to disturb her."

There was a rustle of silk skirts at the door as a tall, fashionably dressed woman entered. "If this is regarding my daughter, I *want* to be disturbed." She was attractive, in spite of the eyes swollen from crying. Her blonde hair was turning white at the temples and some fine creases appeared across her forehead, but neither detracted from her beauty.

As she sat next to Mrs. Gordon, the difference was striking. Aged about the same, Mrs. Gordon looked tired even though her eyes were not affected by tears. The creases around her downturned mouth and between her eyebrows suggested she frowned a lot. Unlike the newcomer, Mrs. Gordon wore a white cap covering much of her hair, and her brown outfit didn't have a single stitch of embroidery embellishing it. Her only extravagance was a silver brooch in the shape of a cross attached to the gown's high neckline at her throat.

Her husband was quite dapper by comparison. Indeed,

if I had to pick the married couple in the room, I'd have paired him with his sister-in-law. He seemed to take pride in his thick, dark hair, wearing it swept up into a wave at the front with the help of pomade. Unlike most men his age, he still had impressive locks. His clothes, too, were modish with a thin pinstripe through the dark blue wool, and a gold stag's head pinned to his tartan cravat. It must be his clan's crest. I'd seen cheap versions of similar pins in the souvenir seller's cart at the station.

"This is my sister-in-law, Mrs. Buchanan," Mrs. Gordon said in a soft Scottish accent. "Her late husband was my brother. She and Juliette have lived alone in Aberdeen since his death several years ago." It was a rather mechanical account, but I couldn't tell if she felt no emotion toward her brother and his family or she was steeling herself against too much emotion.

Oscar introduced us again and restated the reason for our visit. All three expressed their eagerness to help us in any way, but Mrs. Buchanan became upset. She pressed a handkerchief to her nose as tears welled in her eyes.

"Thank you for assisting the police," she said, her voice cracking. "The detective in charge of the investigation didn't seem particularly competent."

"I say," Mr. Gordon protested in an English accent. "He's doing his best."

Mrs. Buchanan's lips pinched but she didn't respond.

"Can you tell us why Juliette was staying with you?" Miss Wheeler asked the Gordons.

"She wrote to us expressing a strong desire to visit.

Mrs. Gordon and I were happy to have her. She's my wife's only family, after all."

"Had she written to you much before?"

"From time to time," Mrs. Gordon said.

Although she hadn't looked at Mrs. Buchanan, Juliette's mother nevertheless seemed to take the lack of correspondence as an accusation directed at her. "She would have written more if *you'd* written to *her*."

"What changed?" I asked before the two women could blame one another for not writing.

Mrs. Gordon touched the silver cross brooch. "We received a letter from her last month begging us to allow her to visit."

"She didn't *beg*," Mrs. Buchanan said testily.

Her sister-in-law stiffened. "It was strongly worded, asking us if we would have her for a while. Of course we agreed, despite our reservations."

"What reservations?" Mrs. Buchanan asked. Apparently this was news to her, too.

Mrs. Gordon clasped her hands together on her lap. "We didn't know what to do with her once she arrived. We live quietly, and Juliette was always such a lively girl when she was young."

"She isn't a child anymore," her mother pointed out.

"Precisely. How would dull, childless people like us entertain her? We don't know any other young people except the local curate, nor do we go to social events. I could take her to church, but would she want to go? We worried that Juliette would be bored."

I understood their view. As someone who also led a quiet life, I wouldn't know what to do with a lively young woman thrust into the midst of my life either. I'd be quite nervous to suddenly play host to one.

"Why was she so insistent?" Oscar asked.

"She wrote that she wanted to get to know us better," Mrs. Gordon said. "I am her late father's sister, after all, so I suppose she hoped I could tell her more about him."

Mrs. Buchanan rolled her eyes. "Juliette thought Edinburgh would be more interesting than Aberdeen. I don't know how she got that into her head, but she suddenly thought life with me rather ordinary and hoped a change of scene would offer something more."

"Suddenly?" Miss Wheeler prompted. "Did something happen to plant the idea in her head to come to Edinburgh?"

"What do you mean?"

"Did she meet someone who urged her to come, or did someone write to her?"

All three frowned at Miss Wheeler. "Write to her," Mrs. Gordon echoed. "Are you suggesting my niece wanted to come to Edinburgh to meet someone? That she was carrying on a secret affair after her arrival, right under our noses?"

"Of course she's not implying that," her husband said. "Are you, Miss Wheeler?"

"Juliette snuck out of the house at dawn," Miss Wheeler told him firmly.

"She didn't *sneak* out. She went for a walk."

"Without telling anyone? At dawn?"

He sank back into the sofa, rubbing his bearded jaw in thought.

Miss Wheeler turned to Mrs. Buchanan. "Did Juliette have a paramour in Aberdeen?"

Mrs. Buchanan teased the damp handkerchief between her fingers. "No." She blinked rapidly and suddenly looked down at her lap. "She did receive more correspondence than usual of late. It was all from a particular friend but...I had my doubts. The writing on the envelope was masculine, and this friend had never written before. After the first letter, Juliette would pounce on the post when it arrived and immediately retreat to her room if she received anything."

Mrs. Gordon twisted in her seat to regard her sister-in-law better. "What did the letters say?"

"I didn't read them. They were private."

"But if you suspected they were from a man and not her friend, why wouldn't you read them? You could have stopped Juliette coming to Edinburgh."

Mrs. Buchanan burst into tears. "Don't you think I've realized that?"

Mrs. Gordon patted her sister-in-law's shoulder, only for Mrs. Buchanan to jerk away. Mrs. Gordon snatched her hand back as if it had been slapped. "Are you suggesting someone wrote to Juliette in Aberdeen, lured her to Edinburgh, then lured her outside to the garden to kidnap her?"

"It's a possibility," Oscar said.

"There's no evidence those letters are linked to her disappearance," Mr. Gordon pointed out. "Indeed, there's no evidence they even led her to come here."

"Are the letters still in Aberdeen?" I asked Mrs. Buchanan.

She nodded as she dabbed at her eyes with her handkerchief. "I left in such a hurry yesterday after receiving the telegram about Juliette's disappearance that I didn't make the connection with the letters until I arrived."

"Juliette may have brought them," Miss Wheeler said. "That's what I'd do if the letter writer was dear to me."

"The police have searched her room," Mr. Gordon said. "As have we. No letters were found."

"May we look?" Oscar asked. "Another search can't hurt."

"Of course," both Mrs. Buchanan and Mrs. Gordon said. They studiously avoided looking at one another before Mrs. Gordon rose. "I'll show you the way."

We were joined by Mr. Gordon and Mrs. Buchanan, too. Fortunately, Juliette's bedroom was a sizeable one and we comfortably fit. While Oscar and I searched under watchful gazes, Miss Wheeler continued to question them.

"We understand that Juliette had just discovered her magical powers."

Mrs. Buchanan nodded. "She inherited it from my side, although I'm artless."

Mrs. Gordon touched her brooch. "We didn't know my sister-in-law's family were magicians."

"I didn't know either," Mrs. Buchanan snapped. "Not

until recently. A cousin informed me that it ran in the family."

"Her family was in trade," Mrs. Gordon added.

"Three generations ago!" Mrs. Buchanan huffed, frustrated. "My cousin told me a spell that he'd found in our grandmother's things years ago. He and I both tried it and nothing happened, but when Juliette spoke the words while holding a woolen hat, the fibers strengthened. They became unbreakable. Neither a sharp pair of scissors nor a knife could cut them. She was excited by the discovery."

"Indeed," Mrs. Gordon said tightly. "Her first letter to us mentioned it. A lot."

"Did she have any plans to use her magic?" Miss Wheeler asked.

"Use it how?" Juliette's mother asked.

"To start a business, or work in a wool mill."

Mr. Gordon wrinkled his nose. "Good lord, no. She's a young lady, not a factory worker."

"Some young ladies wish to work to earn their independence."

"Not my daughter." Mrs. Buchanan frowned then added, "Not that I know of."

"She wasn't in need of money," Mrs. Gordon said. "My brother left his widow quite well-off."

Mrs. Buchanan echoed her sister-in-law's words. "Juliette didn't need money."

Miss Wheeler watched Oscar as he knelt on the floor in front of the fireplace and peered up the chimney. "Independence is not always about money," she murmured, somewhat absently.

A distant clock chimed the hour. Mrs. Gordon touched her husband's arm and gazed up at him. "I have to go. Will you change your mind, just this once, my dear? For Juliette?"

He shook his head and turned away. "Anything, Mr. Barratt?"

"Nothing, but we haven't finished yet." Oscar signaled for me to help him move a chest of drawers.

Mrs. Gordon sighed. "I'm going to the kirk. There's a special service to pray for Juliette's return. And for the maid, too."

The tension between the three seemed to ratchet up a notch. Ordinarily I'd mind my own business, but the situation was dire. I was extremely worried about both missing women and if the tension had anything to do with the disappearances, I thought it best to crack that particular shell and see what spilled out.

After moving the chest of drawers, I dusted off my hands while Oscar inspected the floorboards where it had stood. "You're not going with your wife, Mr. Gordon?" I asked.

"No."

"My husband and I don't share the same faith," Mrs. Gordon said, her voice snippy, "and my sister-in-law is a heathen."

Mrs. Buchanan threw up her hands. "I am *not* a heathen, as well you know. I attend service every Sunday back home, but I want to be here in case there's news of Juliette."

"If you put your trust in God, He will bring her home to us."

Mrs. Buchanan gathered up her skirts. "I prefer to put my trust in the people investigating her disappearance." She spun around with a snap of her skirts and strode out of the room.

A moment later, Mrs. Gordon left, too.

Miss Wheeler helped Oscar and I with the search, but we found nothing. If Juliette brought the mysterious letters with her from Aberdeen, she must have kept them on her person. The letters had to be behind Juliette's desire to come to Edinburgh, I was quite sure of it. The timing was too coincidental for it to be otherwise.

As we left the bedchamber with Mr. Gordon, I asked him if Juliette had met anyone since her arrival in Edinburgh.

"No," he said. "She'd only been here two days."

"Did she seem eager to go out? Did she often go for walks, for example?"

"Only the once before her kidnap, and not alone. The maid who accompanied her was questioned by us and the police and she assured us all that Juliette didn't stop to speak to a soul. Why would she when she didn't know anyone here except my wife and me?"

The footman known as Jack worked at a different house on Moray Place, according to Agnes, but that didn't mean he hadn't slipped messages to Juliette through a member of staff in this household. "Had she made friends with any of the servants?" I asked.

"I don't know," he said, frowning. "Certainly not among our staff, anyway."

"Are you suggesting she made friends with the staff of other households?" Oscar asked.

"I'm afraid I don't know."

"Presumably her maid was questioned about Juliette's acquaintances."

"She didn't have her own maid. Two of the female staff shared the extra work that came with having a young lady in the house. They've been questioned thoroughly by the police, as have the rest of the staff. I assure you, they'd have been found out by now if they were in any way a party to the abduction."

We returned downstairs where Mr. Gordon told the butler to show us out. "Please don't hesitate to ask more questions if you think of them," he said. "We are all eager to have Juliette back."

He returned upstairs while the butler led us to the front door. Mrs. Buchanan stood there, waiting, the damp handkerchief pressed to her nose.

"I'm sorry for leaving the room suddenly," she told us. "My sister-in-law's zealotry tries my patience." Her face crumpled and she pressed the handkerchief to her mouth while she composed herself. After drawing in a deep breath, she continued, "She believes prayer will bring Juliette back. I'm more pragmatic. Anyway, I need to be here at the moment."

"We understand," Miss Wheeler said gently. "Do you mind if I ask one more question?"

"Go ahead."

"Do you know anyone named Jack?"

She blinked in surprise. "No one we're particularly close to, and certainly no one with a close connection to Juliette. Why?"

"It's a line of inquiry."

Oscar addressed the butler who'd busied himself retrieving hats and gloves to allow us to speak to Mrs. Buchanan in private. "It's Anderson, isn't it? Can you account for your whereabouts at the time of Juliette's abduction?"

"I was asleep in the room I've been sharing with the coachman since a leak rendered my bedchamber uninhabitable. The floor creaks dreadfully and we are both light sleepers and would have heard if the other got out of bed. Before you ask, there are no other male members of staff here. The police have already asked this information, sir."

The testy response didn't put Oscar off his interrogation. "Are you familiar with the footman named Jack who works at number eight?"

"No, sir."

He opened the door for us, but Mrs. Buchanan had more to say. "I know you think Juliette ran off with a man."

"It's just a line of inquiry," Miss Wheeler repeated.

"Yes, but..." Mrs. Buchanan tapped the damp handkerchief bunched in her fist against her chest. "My daughter was taken against her will. Perhaps she was lured outside by someone she was corresponding with, but she certainly didn't leave the garden willingly with that person."

"Why do you say that?"

"For one thing, there's a witness who heard her cry out. For another, she left this behind." She removed a bundle of soft butter-yellow wool no bigger than my smallest finger from up her sleeve. "It's wool that was used to make the hair of her favorite doll when she was a child. She keeps it with her, always, and has done so for years. Even before she discovered she was a wool magician, she kept this in the pocket of the outfit she was wearing. It's her good luck charm. It may have fallen out of her pocket in a scuffle, but I think it's more likely she left it behind for me to find, as a message, of sorts."

Oscar held out his palm. "May I?"

Mrs. Buchanan placed the bundle in his hand. He briefly touched it before giving it back. "There's magic in it."

"Oh," she murmured through her tears.

Anderson handed hats and gloves to Oscar and me and gave Miss Wheeler her umbrella. We started to leave when Mrs. Buchanan grasped my arm.

"Please find my daughter," she said, the tears streaming down her cheeks.

I wanted to promise her. I wanted very much to assure her Juliette would be found alive and well and be home by nightfall. But it wasn't in my power to make such a promise. "We'll do everything we can," I said instead.

It felt woefully inadequate.

As we headed down the steps to the pavement, I was keenly aware that we were no closer to finding the two missing women. Not only that, I also couldn't think where we should go next.

Fortunately, Oscar and Miss Wheeler had an idea. With nothing but an earnest look exchanged between them, they strode off along the pavement together.

CHAPTER 11

I used to find it odd that footmen were employed largely for their looks, not their ability, until I learned that their tasks were minimal compared to a maid's, and easy at that. They were somewhat unnecessary to the functioning of a household except, perhaps, at dinner or parties when they were required to serve. I'd also learned that a handsome, tall footman was more desirable than a short, plain one, and so could demand a higher wage. Their appearance was a reflection on the employer's wealth.

If the main function of a footman was to make the household look good, then the one named Jack at number eight Moray Place was an excellent choice. He was taller than Oscar and exceptionally handsome, with thick dark hair, clean-shaven square jaw and broad shoulders. The blue eyes took in the three of us standing on the doorstep but lingered a little longer on Miss Wheeler than Oscar or me. Perhaps that was because she was the one to ask him if he was Jack. Or perhaps it was because she was strikingly pretty herself.

"I am Jack," he said in a voice so deep it seemed to come from the depths of his soul.

"We're assisting the police with their inquiries into the disappearances of Juliette and Mary."

Those blue eyes sharpened. "It's nothing tae do with me! I've never met either of them. In the case of the maid, I've never even seen her. Although I once met the Gordons' niece, that was years ago when I first came tae work here and she was visiting her aunt and uncle. She must have been nae more than fifteen or sixteen. She called here one afternoon with her aunt, but that was the extent of our interactions. I dinnae even know she was back in Edinburgh. Why would I?"

"We found letters addressed to Mary from a man named Jack," Miss Wheeler went on. "Did you write them?"

"Nae! I told ye, their disappearances are nothing tae do with me. When that maid was taken, I was working here. There was a dinner party, and my presence was required the entire time. As for the abduction of the Gordons' niece, all I can say is that I was asleep, but I am not at liberty tae tell you whose bed I was in. That explanation will have tae suffice, for the sake of the lady's reputation. Might I add, you could have verified this with the police before coming here as I've already given that account tae them. Now, unless there are any more questions, I bid ye good day."

He closed the door in our faces without waiting for a reply.

Oscar trotted back down the stairs. "He'll make butler one day with that attitude."

"I believe him," I said. "A young man as handsome as that doesn't need to write to housemaids or use clandestine measures to lure women. He could simply crook his finger and they'd run in his direction."

"You sound enamored, Gavin," Oscar said with a hint of wickedness in his voice.

"Oscar," I hissed.

"It's all right if you are."

"It's not all right!" The conversation was heading in a direction I didn't want to go in. "Anyway, I was *objectively* pointing out that he is handsome. Anyone with eyes can see it."

"I'm not so sure," Miss Wheeler chimed in. Her voice also held a hint of wickedness in it, but I couldn't think why. "His features were certainly arranged well, but I personally didn't find him all that attractive. He was *too* handsome."

"Is there such a thing?" Oscar asked.

"Oh, yes. A little roughness around the edges is far more appealing. Don't you agree, Professor?"

"I wouldn't know." If they were trying to tease a declaration out of me, I wasn't going to take the bait. Besides, I wasn't sure what I'd declare. My romantic interests were a conundrum, even to me.

I changed the subject before Oscar or Miss Wheeler

decided to continue their interrogation. "If Jack the footman didn't write the letters and didn't abduct either woman, that leaves one other Jack from this area. Or, rather, John—Redmayne. I propose we attempt to question him again."

They agreed, but unfortunately Mr. Kinloch had decided to give his butler the afternoon off.

"He was upset by your accusations, so he's gone for a walk," Mr. Kinloch informed us on the doorstep. He went to close the door, only to stop. "I know you and the police need to exhaust every avenue of inquiry, but you're barking up the wrong tree. I know Redmayne well. He's a good man. He'd never harm anyone, let alone a woman."

"Then you won't have a problem giving us the address of his former employer so we can confirm your opinion," Oscar said. "If their account of Redmayne echoes yours, then we'll leave him alone."

Mr. Kinloch hesitated. "Is that a promise?"

"I give my word as a gentleman."

"I'd rather yours, Professor."

I stared at him. "Oh. I can assure you, Oscar's word is as good as mine."

"He's a journalist." Mr. Kinloch indicated a fellow lounging against the garden fence opposite, his hat pulled low. While there was no way to be sure he was a journalist who'd escaped being moved on by the police, on the balance of it, he probably was. "I'm not inclined to like journalists very much at the moment," Mr. Kinloch added.

He cast Oscar an apologetic look but didn't back down from his sentiment.

"Very well," I said, "I give my word, too."

"As do I," Miss Wheeler chimed in. "Since the word of a woman is equally as good as that of a man."

Mr. Kinloch opened the door wider. "Do come in while I look through my paperwork."

We waited in the entrance hall, alone. There was very little to look at, considering the paintings had been removed. The longer we waited, the more my thoughts wandered. The direction of them took me on a different course altogether. One that Oscar and Miss Wheeler seemed to have forgotten.

When Mr. Kinloch returned, he handed a piece of paper to Oscar. "It's nearby. I believe the gentleman has died, but his widow still lives there."

Miss Wheeler left with Oscar behind her, but I lingered. I indicated the bare walls with the imprints left behind by the removed paintings. "It's a shame you had to sell off your family portraits." According to Redmayne, Mr. Kinloch hadn't sold the paintings, but I wanted to hear his response. I wanted to see if it matched the butler's.

Mr. Kinloch followed my gaze. "How did you know they were family portraits?"

"It's often the location for such things, in my experience."

"You may be right about that, but you're wrong about selling them. They're being appraised and cleaned in London."

Appraised *and* cleaned? Redmayne had mentioned the former but not the latter. Was that significant?

Whether it was or not, Mr. Kinloch hadn't taken the bait I'd dangled in front of him. He'd not said the paintings were sold because he was in financial difficulty. I suppose I hadn't expected him to, but I felt I had to try. Someone had stolen the book from my room last night and Mr. Kinloch may well have been the thief. I hadn't ruled him out. However, financial gain was an increasingly unlikely motive. For one thing, he could have sold the book to Mr. Defoe for a much greater sum, and secondly, it seemed he hadn't sold the paintings for financial gain. Of course, he may simply have told Redmayne to use that story with anyone who asked about them, then repeated it himself. I wouldn't eliminate him just yet.

But I knew a way to do so, once and for all.

I returned my hat to my head, touched the brim in farewell, and left.

* * *

THE RESIDENCE of Redmayne's former employer was just as grand as Mr. Kinloch's house, although the street itself wasn't quite as exclusive as Moray Place. The butler invited us inside after checking to see if Mrs. Carter was home for callers, but Miss Wheeler didn't step inside ahead of Oscar and me, as was usual. She scanned the street. Both sides were lined with townhouses, unlike Moray Place where there were buildings only on one side, the other occupied by the garden where Juliette was walking at the time of her abduction.

"Is something the matter?" Oscar asked her.

"I...I'm not sure." She shrugged and entered the house. Oscar's gaze swept the street before he followed her.

Swathed in black from head to toe, with jet jewelry and a black cap covering her white hair, the elderly Mrs. Carter was a picture of respectable widowhood. Despite it being almost one o'clock in the afternoon, the heavy curtains were closed. The only light came from gas lamps positioned on two of the tables, neither placed near her. I wondered what she did all day, since it wasn't enough light for her to read by or do needlepoint.

It became clear, however, that she was so frail she probably did nothing. She breathed heavily, and the hovering maid explained that her mistress found talking at length difficult.

"We'll keep it brief," Oscar assured them both. He explained that we were assisting the police in the search for the missing women and that one of the suspects was her former footman, Redmayne, who'd left her employment to take a position as butler at Mr. Kinloch's home.

Mrs. Carter became quite agitated at the mention of his name and began to cough. The maid hurried to her side and pressed a teacup into her mistress's hands.

Mrs. Carter sipped and seemed to be better for it. "Redmayne is a good man. He wouldn't harm anyone."

"Wasn't he implicated in the abduction of your maid?"

She tapped her hand against her chest as she struggled to draw a breath. "Only because he was courting her and couldn't prove he was asleep in his own bed when she went missing." She paused to draw in two shuddery breaths. "The poor girl was found a few days later, dead."

"Do you have a theory on who killed her?"

Again, Mrs. Carter shook her head. "I think I know *why*, though." She used two hands to lift the teacup to her lips. She took another sip before lowering it. "The girl used to tell people she could do magic."

"This was years ago, wasn't it?" Oscar asked.

"When most magicians hid themselves away, yes. But the silly girl didn't hide like the others. She boasted that she could do such fine needlework because she was a cotton magician."

Cotton! Just like Mary.

Mrs. Carter drew in a deep, steady breath before continuing. "Few folk knew about magicians then, so we all thought she was touched in the head. I suppose there were some who believed her..." She coughed lightly. "One of them must have taken her."

I couldn't see how a maid who had no plans to start a business, living in a time when magic wasn't widely known, could be a threat to anyone. "But why?" I asked. "Financial gain?"

"I suspect someone wanted to eliminate witches. A modern day Witchfinder General, so to speak."

I suppressed my sigh, not wanting her to hear my disappointment. I'd hoped for a new theory that would explain the disappearances, not something she'd gleaned from the latest sensationalist article in the local newspaper.

"I didn't think about it until magicians came out of hiding," she went on. "Then I began to wonder if the girl's boasting had been her downfall. Now those other girls are missing...the two witches from Moray Place."

"Magicians," Miss Wheeler corrected her.

"Yes, of course. Forgive me. It's difficult to change at my age." Mrs. Carter began to cough again.

It was our signal to leave, but Oscar hadn't quite finished. He waited for the coughing fit to end, then asked Mrs. Carter why Redmayne took a position at Mr. Kinloch's house.

"Because the position of butler became available there," she said, matter-of-factly.

"How did he hear about the position?" Oscar asked.

"Through my friend. She was visiting and saw how melancholy Redmayne was. She suggested he make a clean start away from the painful memories of his sweet lassie. I agreed, even though it meant losing a fine footman. She knew Mr. Kinloch wanted a butler and offered to speak to him on Redmayne's behalf."

"And the name of your friend?"

"Mrs. Gordon. She's a neighbor of Mr. Kinloch's. I knew her from our kirk. I don't go anymore. This blasted cough..." She struggled to finish her sentence before another coughing fit gripped her.

We thanked her and the butler saw us out.

"What do you think?" I asked as we walked away.

Miss Wheeler didn't seem to be listening as she glanced back over her shoulder along the street.

"I think Mrs. Buchanan may have inadvertently given us a piece of the puzzle earlier," Oscar said. "She told us her sister-in-law was a zealot. If Mrs. Carter mentioned her maid's claims of being a magician to her friend, Mrs. Gordon may have taken it upon herself to eliminate someone she considered sinful—a witch. The same with the two new abductions."

The thought was chilling, but I didn't think it a valid theory. "Do you honestly believe Mrs. Gordon is that cruel? That mad? She'd have to be unhinged to commit such a dreadful crime against innocent young women, one of whom is her own niece."

Oscar's lips formed a grim line. "I have less faith in humanity than you, Gavin. What do you think, Miss Wheeler?"

She turned to glance over her shoulder again. "I think we're being followed."

Oscar and I both looked behind us.

Then an enormous boom rang out over the city.

CHAPTER 12

My shock was met with amusement from passersby. Even Miss Wheeler chuckled, although her gaze held sympathy.

She looped her arm through mine. "It's just the cannon, Professor."

"Cannon?"

"A sixty-four pounder. It's fired every day at one PM from the castle's battery." She indicated the direction of Edinburgh castle. "You didn't know?"

"We only arrived late yesterday." So had she, but she'd done her research, apparently. I felt like a fool for not doing mine. "Oscar, did you know?"

Oscar stared into the distance as he absently stroked his earlobe. He seemed not to have heard me. It was as if the cannon fire had dazed him.

"Oscar?" I said. "It was just the castle's gun. Nothing to worry about."

He frowned. "Yes, of course. Just the castle's gun." He shrugged and continued walking.

Miss Wheeler and I fell into step alongside him. Before arriving at Mrs. Carter's house, I'd suggested calling at Waverley Station to confirm if Mr. Kinloch and Redmayne were telling the truth about the destination of his paintings—or if they were sent to London at all. If they were, they'd go via rail. Surely a porter or other employee would remember valuable paintings passing through. Such packages wouldn't be loaded onto the trains every day.

It wasn't far and the weather was pleasant. Once my heart stopped racing from the shock of the cannon fire, and once Oscar emerged from his dazed state, it was an enjoyable walk. I liked that Miss Wheeler continued to hold onto my arm, although it was to Oscar that she often glanced.

I leaned closer and whispered in her ear that he was currently not involved with anyone. "Are you, Miss Wheeler? Involved with anyone, that is?"

"That's a complicated question, Professor."

"It shouldn't be."

Oscar heard me that time. "Are you two talking about me?"

Miss Wheeler scoffed. "Not everything is about you, Mr. Barratt."

"Sometimes it is." He flashed her a grin. "And please call me Oscar."

"No."

"I think we've earned the right to call one another by our first names."

"It's not a privilege that can be earned, Mr. Barratt. It can be bestowed, but only when the time is right."

His face fell and he sighed. "I'm afraid we don't have time. Once this is over, you'll go your way and we'll go ours, never to meet again. Unless—"

"No," she said, most emphatically.

"You haven't heard my proposal yet."

"I don't need to. I already know it's not something that will interest me."

"You can't possibly know that without hearing it."

She tapped a gloved finger to her lower lip in mock thought. "Let me see... Were you going to suggest I leave Mr. Defoe's employ and come and work for your patrons, Lord and Lady Rycroft, and assist you and Professor Nash in stocking their library, even though the task can be accomplished without me?"

"I may have been," Oscar mumbled.

"And were you going to make that suggestion because you believe I need rescuing from Mr. Defoe?"

"He's a boorish, arrogant, power-hungry, selfish man."

"You forgot to mention rich. He pays me very well. Tell me, Mr. Barratt, would your employers pay me enough to afford the fine clothes you see me wearing?"

Oscar's gaze traveled the length of her. When it returned to her face, his eyes held a spark of desire. He'd liked what he'd seen. "I suppose you do have a rather impressive trunk."

My face heated. "Oscar!"

He blinked innocently at me. "I was referring to the size of her luggage."

I pushed my glasses up my nose. "Yes, of course, but it could be misconstrued."

Miss Wheeler laughed lightly as she tightened her hold on my arm. "It's all right, Professor. I'm used to poor attempts at flirtation from men like Mr. Barratt."

Oscar laughed, not put off in the least. "I guarantee you haven't met anyone like me before, Miss Wheeler. Please allow me to apologize for my comment about your trunk." He placed a hand over his chest and bowed from the neck without breaking stride. "Although I am not sorry for attempting to flirt with you. We have limited time together, so I'm grasping every opportunity."

Miss Wheeler lifted her chin. "Why? You hardly know me. I may not be worth the effort."

"I know enough."

Miss Wheeler swallowed heavily, her bold confidence suddenly vanishing. He'd disarmed her with nothing more than a few words and a velvet-soft voice.

"Consider my offer, Miss Wheeler," Oscar went on.

"You haven't made an offer, Mr. Barratt. Even if you could make one on behalf of Lord and Lady Rycroft, I won't take it. I'm comfortable with my decision to remain with Mr. Defoe. The work is varied, he respects me, and he's not as villainous as you think he is."

"Are you certain?"

Miss Wheeler bristled. "Do drop the subject, or I'll be

forced to discontinue our association and investigate without you."

Oscar held up his hands in surrender. "Your wish is my command."

She groaned. "Is he always this insufferable, Professor?"

I smiled. "Only when he's trying too hard to impress."

"You've seen him like this before?" She pouted. "And I thought I was unique."

Oscar shot me a frosty glare.

I bit my lip at my bumbling mistake. "Oh, I...er, yes of course you are, Miss Wheeler. You are a most singular woman. Please forget what I said."

She hugged my arm. "I think we should all refocus on the task at hand. The station is just over there."

The first porter we spoke to did recall the paintings, but suggested our questions would be better answered by the freight company tasked with packing and transporting them. A representative of the company was currently on the furthest platform, overseeing the unloading of packages from a freight carriage. The fellow was happy to talk to us, but only after Miss Wheeler slipped him some money.

"Aye, I remember Kinloch's paintings." He removed his clipboard from under his arm and flipped over the top page. He ran his finger down the columns, stopping at an entry near the bottom. "Here it is. Six in total, all framed. Sent tae Christie's in London."

The auction house!

We all kept our features schooled as we thanked the fellow. It wasn't until we'd left the station altogether that Miss Wheeler broke the silence.

"Kinloch lied."

"As did Redmayne," I said. "He would have known the paintings were destined for auction. It would seem Mr. Kinloch is in financial difficulty, after all."

"Then why not sell the book to Defoe for more money?" Oscar asked.

"Because he was sincere when he said he wanted it housed in a public library, not hidden away in a private collection. Forgive me if I've cast your employer in a poor light, Miss Wheeler."

"There's nothing to forgive, Professor." She pressed a hand to her stomach. "Is anyone else parched? Shall we discuss this over a cup of tea and sandwiches?"

We asked a shoeshine lad if there was a teashop nearby that made good sandwiches, and he gave us convoluted directions that led us down one alley after another. We managed to find it, however, and sat at a table away from the window at Miss Wheeler's insistence.

"What shall we do about Kinloch and Redmayne's lie?" she asked while we waited for our refreshments to arrive.

"It was clearly done to hide Kinloch's financial problems," Oscar said. "Problems that have risen because his rivals have improved their fabrics."

"Thanks to magicians who possess the same magical craft as Mary and Juliette. So, either Kinloch or Redmayne killed them out of anger over Kinloch's floundering business, or kidnapped them because they want to use them to improve the quality of the fabrics Kinloch's factory produces."

Both theories were heinous and stole my appetite, but I didn't believe the latter one. "If he wants to compete with magician-owned factories, he could just employ a magician. There's no need to kidnap them and force them to work for him."

"It is rather an extreme motive," she agreed. "But so is the alternative. That he has killed them out of misguided jealousy or perceived rivalry. Mr. Barratt, you claim to be such a good judge of character, do you think Kinloch is disturbed enough to go to such lengths to save his own business?"

Oscar watched the waitress as she carried a tray of tea things toward us. "Not Kinloch. But I could see Redmayne being that disturbed." He waited for the waitress to set the tray down and distribute cups. Once she was gone, he continued in a low voice. "Remember that his deceased lover claimed to be a magician. If her claim led to them falling out, he could have been upset enough to kidnap and kill her. Then, years later, Mary moves into his neighborhood. She also claims to be a magician, triggering some dark, twisted part of him that is compelled to remove her. Juliette, too."

I stared at him, horrified. What dark, twisted part of Oscar had conjured up that theory?

Miss Wheeler seemed less disturbed than me by this side of him. "It's certainly a possibility," she said as she poured the tea into our cups. "It's more viable than Kinloch doing it."

"No!" I looked from one to the other, incredulous. "It isn't a possible theory. Surely not. Redmayne isn't the friendliest fellow, but that doesn't mean he's a murderer."

"We have to keep an open mind," Oscar said.

"Do we?" I shook my head. "I just don't see it. Not kidnap. Or murder, for that matter."

"What does a kidnapper and murderer look like?"

I picked up my teacup. "I'll let you know when I see one."

Miss Wheeler cast a sympathetic gaze at me. "Professor, it's a commendable trait to think well of everyone. I wish I was like you. Alas, I have seen evil lurk in the hearts of people others call good. Some hide that dark side of themselves very well, and it's not until they lower their guard that it's exposed. You are fortunate that it's rarely exposed to you."

Meaning it had been exposed to her often. As a dark-skinned woman, I didn't doubt it. In the short space of time we'd been together, I'd seen the way some people looked at her. I couldn't begin to imagine what she'd experienced in her lifetime. Oscar and I had faced evil in the form of Lord Coyle, but Miss Wheeler might have faced it much more frequently.

I felt foolish for being so naïve. "I apologize, Miss Wheeler. You're right. Redmayne may be hiding his true nature. Kinloch, too."

"We shall see," was all she said.

* * *

I hoped stopping for a light luncheon hadn't been our downfall, giving our suspects time to make new plans to cover their tracks. If Mr. Kinloch or Redmayne somehow learned that we'd made inquiries at the station about the paintings, they might move to create false alibis to throw us off their trail.

I was about to mention this when a flash of metal in the shadowy recess further along the alley caught my eye. At that moment, a gunshot rang out.

I dropped to the pavement, but Oscar and Miss Wheeler did the opposite. They ran toward the recess. I was about to shout at them to take cover when I realized the gunman had left his hiding place and was running toward the bright daylight at the exit of the lane. Even so, it was madness to chase him.

My worst fear came to fruition. The gunman raised his arm and aimed the gun over his shoulder at his pursuers.

"Oscar!" I cried.

Oscar dove at Miss Wheeler, slamming her into the brick wall. It may have saved both their lives if the gunman had fired another shot. He did not. Two people entered the alley ahead of him. He ran straight past them, and neither took any notice of him as they laughed at a shared joke.

"Idiot!" Miss Wheeler shoved Oscar. "Move out of the way!"

In a swift, practiced act that took less than a moment,

she'd removed a leather pouch from her skirt pocket, whipped off her right glove, and dipped her bare hand into the pouch. She removed a fistful of something, then spoke some words that I couldn't hear as she opened her fist. White dust lifted off her palm and darted after the gunman.

No, not dust. Chalk. She was a chalk magician.

Oscar ran to the end of the alley only to stop at the exit. He shook his head and waited for Miss Wheeler and me to join him.

I picked up his hat and her umbrella on my way—both forgotten in the excitement—and ran to catch up to Miss Wheeler. "Are you all right?" I asked her.

"Yes, yes." She'd already returned the pouch of chalk dust to her pocket and was in the process of thrusting her hand back into her glove. So that was why she wore them at all times. She couldn't go around with chalk on her hands. Indeed, the fact that she kept chalk dust on her in anticipation of using it as a weapon was wise.

She continued past Oscar, her strides purposeful. "Hurry along, both of you. We have him now."

Oscar and I exchanged glances. Then we trailed after her, dodging tourists and other pedestrians ambling along the Royal Mile, until we finally caught up to her as she passed a tobacconist shop. I wasn't sure she noticed us. Her singular focus was dead ahead, yet no matter how much I strained to look, I couldn't see anyone who looked suspicious. Indeed, what was I even looking for? The gunman was neither short nor tall and had worn men's clothing. There was nothing to distinguish him from the hundreds of others in the busy vicinity.

"Can you see your chalk dust on someone's clothing?" I asked her.

She didn't respond, too intent was she on her quarry.

"I doubt it reached him," Oscar said, his tone apologetic. "I'm sorry I pushed you out of the way, Miss Wheeler. I didn't know what you had planned. I didn't know you were a chalk magician. If you'd told us—"

She put up a hand to stop him. "It doesn't matter."

"Then slow down."

"Do you want your umbrella?" I held it out to her.

"Not yet." She lifted her face, as if feeling the air on her cheeks and nose, then suddenly turned into a side street.

Oscar had watched her, frowning, but now his face cleared. "You weren't trying to dust his clothes with it, were you?"

"No," she said. "I was trying to create a trail to follow him."

"But we can't see the chalk," I said.

"You can't, but I can. Well, I can sense it, is perhaps a better way of putting it."

"Impressive," Oscar said.

"No thanks to you," Miss Wheeler shot back. "I almost didn't get the chance."

"I didn't know you could send a chalk dust trail to follow a particular target, let alone follow that invisible trail."

"Not invisible. Not to me."

Oscar didn't seem cross at being chastised. Indeed, he continued to glance at Miss Wheeler as he kept pace with her. It was clear he was impressed by her skill, perhaps even in awe of her. I also suspected he was wondering if he could incorporate any of the words from her spell into his ink one. He could make his ink float, but as far as I was aware, he couldn't make it follow someone and then follow its trail merely by using his magical sense.

There were fewer people in the side street but it was still busy, being so close to the Royal Mile. I couldn't make out who we were following, but Miss Wheeler didn't break stride. She was confident we were heading in the right direction, and that boosted my confidence. The swift pace was beginning to take its toll on me, however. My breathing was more labored, my brow damp at the hairline. I removed my hat so it didn't become sweaty at the band. My two companions didn't seem to be affected.

"I knew it!" Oscar touched his right ear. "I felt something pass my ear when the cannon went off. I think it was a bullet. The shooter must have timed their shot with the cannon."

Good lord. If the bullet hadn't missed... Oscar could have... I reached out a hand to grasp onto him lest I succumb to the dizziness that suddenly overwhelmed me.

"Why didn't you say something?" Miss Wheeler asked Oscar.

"You distracted me."

"How?"

"You asked me to take a good look at you. Anyway, it

was you who said you knew someone was following us, so I'm not the only one who didn't act on their instincts."

"At least I mentioned it."

I cleared my throat to get their attention. "Er, may we concentrate, please. Miss Wheeler, do you still have the chalk's scent?"

"I do." She pointed down another lane and we all headed that way, our pace somewhere between a rapid walk and a trot. We turned again, and I could have sworn we were heading back to the Royal Mile.

"Considering you thought we were being followed after we left Mr. Kinloch's residence, he should be our number one suspect." I sucked in a breath to steady my nerves and refill my lungs. I wasn't used to so much exertion. "Redmayne wasn't there, so we can exclude him."

"We only have Kinloch's word on that," Oscar pointed out.

Miss Wheeler turned again and headed up a set of stairs that went on and on, eventually narrowing into a covered close. It was so narrow I could stretch out my arms and touch the cool stone walls. The air smelled dank with an underlying putridity of sewage, and I hated to think what was making the cobblestones slippery underfoot.

Miss Wheeler suddenly stopped, raising a finger to silence us even though neither Oscar nor I had uttered a word. The only sound came from my labored breathing. There was no one there.

We'd lost the gunman.

CHAPTER 13

Still reluctant to speak lest I break Miss Wheeler's concentration, I tapped Oscar on the arm to get his attention. I lifted my hands, palms up, in a question. What should we do now? Continue onward, out of the close? Or try one of the doors? We'd passed several on the way up the steps, and there were more in the covered section. As I was considering our options, a door behind us opened and a woman emerged. Her tired eyes watched us with suspicion as her bony fingers gripped the door.

Miss Wheeler went to speak to her and returned moments later. The woman went on her way, basket over her arm.

"Did you ask her if she saw someone?" Oscar asked.

Miss Wheeler shook her head and indicated a wooden door with an iron handle near where we'd stopped. "I asked her what's in there."

"Did the gunman go inside?"

"He did."

"How do you know?" I asked.

"There are faint traces of my chalk dust in the air there and on the doorknob."

"And what did the woman say?"

"She didn't know. She's never seen anyone come or go, but yesterday morning she heard a woman cry out then the door slam. When she emerged from her home to investigate, she didn't see anyone or anything out of the ordinary. She'd always thought the rooms beyond the door were vacant. No one's lived there for years. Apparently the whole building is owned by a vicar."

"Vicar!" I squinted at the door in an attempt to see the chalk dust Miss Wheeler claimed was there, but couldn't see any traces of it among the old scratches and knots in the wood. "We should tell D.I. Smith. He can locate the vicar and fetch a key."

Oscar pointed toward the light at the end of the close. "Good idea, Gavin. Take Miss Wheeler with you."

"Are you going to stay here and watch the door?" I knew Oscar. He could be impetuous and brave, a combination that didn't always have his own best interests at heart. "You won't go in, will you?"

"Just take Miss Wheeler and—" He broke off as she strode up to the door. He rushed after her. "Miss Wheeler, get away from there. You can't go in. It's too dangerous."

She ignored him and tried the doorknob. "Locked."

I blew out a relieved breath. It wasn't just relief for Miss

Wheeler's safety. It was just as much for Oscar's and mine, if I were being honest. I wasn't the bravest soul. The thought of violence made me squeamish and lightheaded. Beyond that door was a gunman who'd already tried to kill us twice. Every part of me screamed to run far away. Thankfully, with the door locked, my companions were forced to accept the situation was hopeless.

Except they didn't.

Miss Wheeler took off her hat and removed two pins from her hair. The arrangement didn't move. She stuck the pins into the lock and twiddled them about until the lock tumbled, then returned the pins to her hair. She straightened and placed the hat back on her head. Just when I thought she couldn't be more remarkable than she already was, she'd produced another trick from up her sleeve. Or her hair in this instance.

Oscar reached for the doorknob and opened the door an inch. Fortunately, the hinges were well oiled and didn't make a sound. He signaled for me to take Miss Wheeler away, but she shook her head.

"I'm not leaving you to face the gunman alone, Mr. Barratt. You need me." She withdrew the pouch of chalk dust from her pocket.

"I can't allow you to put yourself in danger."

"Stop delaying. Time is off the essence. Those poor girls could still be alive in there. I'm going with you and that's that. Professor Nash can fetch the police."

I was about to point out that her chalk magic couldn't compete against a gun, when the door was wrenched wide open from the other side and a figure slammed into Oscar, sending him tumbling into Miss Wheeler. They fell to the ground at my feet in a tangle of limbs. The pouch of chalk landed out of reach, unopened.

"Go after him, Gavin!" Oscar shouted from where he was sprawled on the ground.

Right. It was up to me. I slapped a hand to my hat to stop it falling off and ran after the man, sprinting in the direction we'd come. By the time I reached the long flight of stairs, however, I knew I'd never catch him.

Oscar came up behind me but didn't bother to pursue either. He swore under his breath. "Did you recognize him?"

"No. Miss Wheeler, did you?"

There was no answer. Oscar and I turned to see the door open and Miss Wheeler missing. We exchanged glances then rushed back. I drew in a breath to call out her name, but Oscar stopped me with a finger to his lips. He was right to be cautious. We didn't know if the gunman acted alone.

Blood pounding through my veins, I followed Oscar into the dark room beyond. We seemed to be in the entrance hall of a grand old house, going by the wood paneling on the walls and the carved newel post. Apparently the area around the Royal Mile had been popular with wealthy merchants who built multi-story residences, guild halls, and shops. This must have been one of them. Now it appeared to be a neglected slum tenement languishing in the old part of the city no longer desired by the fashionable and rich.

The single window had been boarded up, but enough light seeped between the cracks, showing the stairs to be too dangerous to navigate. Some were broken, others missing altogether. Miss Wheeler was a few feet ahead of us, moving quietly on the tips of her toes. We followed her across flagstones worn smooth from centuries of use.

I was relieved to see that Miss Wheeler had taken the precaution of removing her right glove. Her hand was closed into a fist, hopefully clutching enough chalk dust to momentarily blind an attacker should one come at us. I glanced at Oscar and was surprised to see he held a small knife. I hadn't known he was carrying one.

We passed the staircase and headed into a bigger room. It was empty of furniture, with more carved wood paneling on both the walls and coffered ceiling, and a fireplace as tall as me with heraldic escutcheons the size of my head chiseled into the stone mantelpiece. An oil lamp and box of matches had been placed on the hearth. As with the stairwell, the windows in this room were boarded up, but enough light filtered through the cracks that I could see the hearth was made of stone, while the floor was wooden boards. They announced our presence with an ominous *creak* when stepped on.

We paused, partly through terror at having made a noise, partly to listen.

But no one shot at us. No one shouted for us to leave or threatened us in any way. We were alone.

Or so I thought.

A faint scuffing sound came from behind one of the walls. Miss Wheeler and Oscar glanced at one another then rushed forward, unconcerned with creaking floorboards or their footsteps echoing in the empty room. Miss Wheeler placed her ear to one of the panels while Oscar pressed another in an attempt to unlatch a hidden door.

I joined them and knocked on one of the panels. Nothing happened.

Oscar knocked, too. We both tapped wall panels, searching for a hollow space behind. Then Miss Wheeler ordered us to shush. She held up a finger as she pressed her ear to the wall. I heard it too. Muffled voices. Female ones.

Oscar and I tapped panels in earnest until I finally hit one that sounded different to the others. I pressed on the wood, but the panel didn't open. Oscar and Miss Wheeler tried, too. Nothing happened. The voices were still muffled, but they were louder and filled with desperation.

"A hammer," Oscar said, looking around. "Something to break through."

There was nothing, not even fire irons on the hearth. Then I saw it. The escutcheons carved into the stone fireplace surround were blackened from years of soot, except for one. It was clean. Too clean.

I pressed both hands to it and pushed. The stone shield sank an inch.

"You got it," Oscar said, still at the wall where one of

the panels had popped open. He opened it wider, revealing a pitch-dark space beyond.

The voices cried out in excitement, but they were still muffled.

"It's all right," Miss Wheeler said, her voice soothing. "We've come to rescue you."

I quickly struck a match and lit the lamp, my fingers fumbling as I replaced the glass chimney over the flame. I handed the lamp to Oscar who led the way inside, Miss Wheeler on his heels, but not for long. She surged past him and fell to her knees in front of one of the women. She removed the gag from the captive's mouth.

Mary—I was sure from her clothing that she was Mary the maid—began to sob. The other woman, dressed in a silk dress, must be Juliette Buchanan. Miss Wheeler removed Juliette's gag, too, but instead of crying she let out a string of abuse directed at her kidnappers. She didn't stop until her hands and feet were freed from their bindings.

"There was more than one?" Oscar asked as he assisted Juliette to her feet, while I helped Mary.

Juliette didn't seem too weakened from her ordeal. Her voice was strong, her eyes flashing in the light of the oil lamp, now held by Miss Wheeler. "There were three—two men and a woman."

"A woman?" Miss Wheeler echoed. "Can you identify any of them?"

"Let's get them home before we pepper them with

questions," I said. "Are you harmed? Do you need to see a doctor?"

"We are not injured," Juliette said, "aside from a few scratches and bruises." She inspected her wrists where the rope had rubbed the flesh raw. Her hair was tangled, as was Mary's, and the hem of her dress had come down. Despite her disarray, there was a bearing about Juliette that commanded attention. "We've received food and water, and they made beds for us. Of sorts." She kicked a bundle of rags and stuffed sacks, which knocked over a night soil bucket. Head held high, she picked up her skirts. "I want to see my mother."

Oscar offered her his arm. She hesitated before taking it and allowed him to assist her from the hidden room. I steered Mary into the lighter, larger room, where her tears finally abated. I patted her hand, unsure what else to do to comfort her. The small gesture brought on a fresh wave of tears.

Juliette put an arm around the maid's shoulders and gave her a little shake. "That's enough now, Mary. We're safe. It's over. These people will take us home and the police will find who did this and punish them. We'll get our justice."

Her no-nonsense determination rallied Mary. The maid wiped her nose on her sleeve. "Not the police, Miss. We cannae trust them."

Juliette gave Mary's shoulders another shake. "We *can*. Those people were not officials. They were operating outside the law."

LAWS OF WITCHCRAFT

"But they said we were on *trial*."

"Trial?" Miss Wheeler echoed. "On what charge?"

Juliette's gaze met hers. "Witchcraft."

CHAPTER 14

"Ignorant, that's what they are," Juliette snarled. "Ignorant, narrow-minded, horrible people. I hope they rot in prison."

"Me too," Mary declared. "Horrible people."

The maid seemed to take strength from Juliette, who showed no ill signs from her captivity. A stark reminder came when both girls shielded their eyes as we emerged into the light. They needed a moment to adjust to the brightness after being held in the dark for so long.

We'd found ourselves on a busy street, but few passersby paid us any attention. Those who did wrinkled their noses at the filthy state of the two women with us. None stopped to ask if they were all right.

I wasn't sure where we were, but Mary, the only local among us, directed us to Moray Place. Oscar spotted two constables walking their patch and informed them we'd found the two kidnapped women. One left to inform the investigative team at police headquarters and the other continued with us to Moray Place. He asked the women to wait for D.I. Smith before discussing their ordeal, but Juliette was in no mood to wait.

"We never saw their faces. They wore masks covering all but their eyes. One was a woman, two others were men. There were no distinguishing features, they weren't tall or short, fat or thin."

"One of the men smelled nice," Mary piped up.

"What did he smell like?" Oscar asked.

"Soap."

The kidnappers had been clever to hide their identity. It could mean they didn't intend to kill the two women, but planned to release them, and didn't want to be identified later.

"You mentioned they put you through a mock trial for witchcraft," I said.

Juliette nodded. "I'm a wool magician."

"I'm a cotton magician," Mary added. "The man who did all the talking told us if we confessed to being witches, they'd let us go."

"They wouldn't have," Juliette growled. "I told Mary to keep quiet. If we'd confessed, they would have meted out punishment. I've studied history. I know what they did to so-called witches. Our kidnappers were mad." She tapped her temple. "They would have done the same to us."

She was right about the troubled history of witchcraft. My studies on the subject had been difficult reading at times.

"They were our judges, jury and executioners," Juliette went on. "Whenever my gag came off, I warned Mary not to tell them anything. She was marvelously courageous."

The maid's face crumpled as fresh tears tumbled down her cheeks. "Ye were the brave one, Miss Buchanan. I couldnae survived in there without ye."

"Yes. Well. We can only do what we can do." Juliette self-consciously fidgeted with her tangled locks, using her arms to hide her face, but not before I saw tears well in her eyes. "I knew we'd be rescued, sooner or later. I'm just glad my uncle didn't wait for the police to do their job and hired private investigators."

None of us corrected her. In a way, it was a kindness for her to think her uncle and aunt had hired us.

"How did you find us?" she asked. We were close to Moray Place now, and both women had quickened their pace, sensing loving embraces weren't far away.

"We interrogated a number of people who knew you," Miss Wheeler said, "and one who claimed not to know either of you, but we believed was a suspect. Someone followed us, then shot at us."

Mary gasped.

"Twice," I added.

She gasped again.

"We managed to follow the gunman after the second shooting," Miss Wheeler went on. "He led us straight to you."

"That was foolish of him," Juliette said, sounding surprised.

"Miss Wheeler is a chalk magician," Oscar clarified. "She threw chalk dust at the gunman, then used her magical senses to follow the chalk trail to the place where you were being held. He didn't know he was being followed."

"Nobody came into the room where we were," Juliette said.

"He must have thought himself safe, only to find us on the doorstep when he reemerged. At that point it was too late to do anything except run. There was no point trying to stop us entering the building. Firing a gun in broad daylight near a busy street could very well lead to his capture, which probably explained why he didn't risk firing a second time outside the teashop. Since neither you nor Mary could identify him, and nor could we, he cut his losses and escaped."

"Coward," Juliette spat.

"You say you can't identify them," Miss Wheeler said, "but would you know their voices?"

"Perhaps we would, but only for the man that did all the talking." Juliette looked to Mary, who nodded. "The other man and the woman never uttered a word. Not once."

"The voice of the man who spoke to you," Miss Wheeler went on, "it wasn't familiar?"

Both women shook their heads.

"Do either of you attend church?"

"I do, in Aberdeen," Juliette said.

Mary bit her lip and lowered her head. "I like my

Sunday mornings off too much tae waste it sitting on hard pews. Is that why they took us? Because we dinnae go tae the kirk?"

Juliette slipped her hand inside Mary's. "That is *not* the reason."

Miss Wheeler also hastily assured them that it wasn't. "The reason I ask is because the building in which you were found is owned by a vicar."

Mary gasped again, but Juliette seemed unsurprised. "I should have known he was a religious crank. He had a self-righteous air about him. He called us unnatural abominations."

"He told me I had the devil in me," Mary added. "He said confessing to being a witch would expel the devil and allow me to serve God better." The girl's chin began to wobble again.

Juliette's thumb caressed Mary's. The simple act bolstered the maid and she managed to hold back her tears.

"We can't be certain if the vicar who owns the building is involved," I cautioned them.

Miss Wheeler agreed. "I thought he might be the vicar at the church where you attend Sunday service, but it seems there's no connection if you've never attended here, Miss Buchanan, and Mary doesn't go at all."

She exchanged glances with Oscar and me. She may be right about the vicar not being involved, but we couldn't discount the religious motive for the crime. Indeed, we knew of another person who was very religious.

Juliette's aunt, Mrs. Gordon.

Was the reason the female kidnapper hadn't uttered a word in the captives' presence because one, or both, would recognize her voice?

It was hard to stomach. Surely not Juliette's own aunt. She possessed a cool, brisk manner, but she'd seemed genuinely worried about her niece. Most families had their problems, and I suspected the death of her brother—Juliette's father—had triggered a distancing between sisters-in-law that went beyond the physical, but it would be cruel indeed to orchestrate her niece's abduction.

Unless she didn't see it as cruelty, but righteous. Was Mrs. Gordon so devout that she put the demands of her faith above the well-being of Juliette?

Juliette turned to Miss Wheeler. "You should look into Jack, the footman at number eight. He's involved." She said it with more vehemence than anything she'd said so far.

"Aye," Mary said, equally vehement. "He dinnae do the kidnapping, mind. Neither man was tall like Jack. But he's involved, the cur. He must be."

"Because he wrote the letters to you both, luring you outside so that you could be taken?" Oscar asked.

"Not just then," Juliette said. "He wrote to me in Aberdeen. He lured me to Edinburgh on a promise of..." She shook her head. "Never mind what. I thought he loved me. He didn't. I'm such a fool for believing him."

"Me too," Mary said. "He fooled us both, the cur."

"Are you certain it's Jack the footman from number

eight?" Oscar asked. "Did he identify himself in the letters?"

"He signed 'em as Jack," Mary hedged. "The butcher's boy is also Jack, but the one in my letters says we've never spoken, so it wasnae him."

For the first time since her rescue, Juliette seemed uncertain, too. She frowned. "His first letter to me said he'd noticed me on my last visit to my aunt and uncle in Edinburgh. He knew it was seven years ago. He said he'd watched me from afar then, and that he knew I'd admired him, but he couldn't act on it. He'd been thinking about me ever since. Who else named Jack would have known I was here back then?"

"*Did* you admire him at the time?" Miss Wheeler asked gently.

"Of course. He is terribly handsome."

"Aye." Mary nodded, sagely. "He's a braw lad, all right."

Juliette tossed her mop of tangled hair. "Anyway, I wanted to visit Edinburgh again. Aberdeen is a little quiet." She grunted, but didn't continue. I suspect she was thinking about the irony of wanting to leave the quiet life only to have too much adventure here in Edinburgh.

We turned onto Moray Place just as it began to rain. Miss Wheeler put up her umbrella and held it over Juliette's head. Mary sidled closer to be protected, too. Juliette released the maid's hand and took her arm instead. The women huddled close.

Juliette's gaze slid to the garden square opposite the

houses. Her nostrils flared and her lips pinched. I wasn't sure if she was upset or furious to be near the location of her abduction again. Either way, she was trying hard to contain her emotions. "I don't know if it matters," she said, "but the man who did the actual kidnapping was the man who never spoke."

"The same with the one who took me," Mary added. "The one who did all the talking waited in the carriage."

We walked past Mr. Kinloch's house. Apart from a constable stationed at the base of the stairs, all was quiet, the curtains drawn. The fellow who'd been lounging against the garden fence earlier was no longer there. The constable accompanying us went up to his colleague and spoke quietly. The other's brows shot up as he stared at Juliette and Mary as if they were sideshow freaks.

Juliette lifted her chin even higher, but Mary didn't seem to notice.

She stopped walking. "Ye ain't going tae find them, are ye?" She appealed to Miss Wheeler, then to Oscar and me. "There's nae clues, is there?" Her breathing quickened and her eyes filled with tears. "What if they do it again?"

It was something that had worried me, too, ever since freeing the girls. Even if Juliette and Mary were vigilant and made sure they were never on their own, there were other magicians. If cleansing the city of so-called witches was the motive, many men and women in Edinburgh could be the next victim.

A sense of hopelessness swamped me, weighing me down. The magicians of Edinburgh needed to be warned.

Juliette, however, proved she was not only stoic and brave, she was also clever. "There may be a way to identify the man who took me from the garden. I managed to slip a piece of wool inside his coat pocket. It holds my magic in it."

My hopes faded. "Your mother found it left in the garden."

"That's different wool. I left that behind deliberately for my family to find, but I also removed one strand and placed it into the kidnapper's pocket during the scuffle. It may still be there. His coat was black and made of heavy wool, suitable for winter. I remember because it was odd to be wearing it in summer."

We needed to check the coats of all our male suspects.

"We'll begin at Kinloch's." Oscar signaled to the two constables to join us. "We'll start with Redmayne."

Miss Wheeler agreed. "Take a constable with you and round up all the coats belonging to Redmayne, Kinloch and Blackburn. I'll take the other constable and check Jack the footman. Professor, escort Mary and Juliette home."

"Why them?" Juliette asked.

"Since you are both local to this street, we focused our investigation here. Blackburn heard you cry out on the morning you were taken, but then retracted his statement. Jack is a suspect because of the letters, and Redmayne is named John. He also worked at a house where another woman disappeared, years ago. She was his lover."

"Who is Redmayne?" Juliette asked.

Miss Wheeler indicated the house where the constable

had been standing guard. "Mr. Kinloch's butler. Mr. Kinloch himself is a suspect because his ancestor was the Witchfinder General."

"That's a tenuous connection, isn't it?"

"It is, but it's one we should follow up, not least because Mr. Kinloch owns a wool mill. He invested heavily in developing a new cotton-wool blend before he knew about magicians. He's artless and his business is now suffering."

The financial motive seemed to make more sense to Juliette than the witchfinder one. "Very well. Everyone meet at my uncle's house. Mary, come with the professor and me, unless you have a particular desire to return to your own home."

Mary followed her gaze to the house where she worked, squeezed between Mr. Kinloch's and the Gordons'. "That ain't my home. I dinnae settle in. I'm going tae resign now and go home tae me ma." She squeezed Juliette's arm. "Thank ye for taking care of me in there. I couldnae survived without ye."

Juliette pressed her lips together and blinked back tears. She drew Mary into a fierce hug. "We took care of each other."

They parted and Mary went on her way, taking the basement stairs down to the service rooms under her employer's house. Someone squealed in delight at the sight of her and I felt satisfied that she'd be all right.

We split into three groups as Miss Wheeler had suggested, with me going to the Gordons' house with Juliette. The door flung open before we reached it and Mrs. Buchanan burst out. She gathered her daughter into a hug as Juliette's wall of bravery finally crumbled and she sobbed in her mother's arms. They stayed like that, despite the rain, until Mrs. Gordon encouraged them inside. She briefly embraced her niece, only to wrinkle her nose as she quickly pulled away.

"Anderson, have a bath drawn for Miss Buchanan," she directed the butler. "Send tea and whatever she'd like to eat up to her room."

"I'm not going to my room yet." Still holding her mother's hand, Juliette swept past her aunt and ascended the grand staircase, every bit the haughty belle of the ball. Dirty clothes and messy hair notwithstanding, she was quite a magnificent sight. The kidnappers might come to regret abducting Juliette Buchanan. "Come along, Professor," she said over her shoulder. "We'll wait in the drawing room."

Mrs. Gordon looked at me. "Wait for what?"

"Some of your neighbors are about to pay a visit," I said.

She glanced at the door then to her butler, who hadn't moved. "Send refreshments into the drawing room. Is Mr. Gordon at home?"

"He's in his study, madam."

"Please inform him his niece has been returned to us."

The butler went to do her bidding, while I followed the Buchanan women up the stairs. When I glanced back, Mrs. Gordon was still standing in the entrance hall. She seemed to be in a daze as she stared directly ahead at the space where the butler had been moments earlier, clutching the silver cross brooch at her throat.

* * *

Jack the footman looked nervous as he stood in the Gordons' drawing room, a coat over his arm. He had good reason to be worried. Although I doubted he was involved, the evidence pointed to him. No one else among the gathered neighbors was named Jack.

John Redmayne came closest. It was quite possible he'd been known as Jack in his youth. In contrast to the footman, Redmayne stood tall and erect, his physical strength on full display as he towered over Blackburn, standing beside him. The coachman was broad, however, and perfectly capable of bundling Juliette and Mary into a waiting carriage.

Mary had changed her mind and decided to come after all, in the company of Agnes, the other maid from her household. Both young women looked out of place in the drawing room in their plain black maid's uniforms. Housemaids would usually only enter the reception rooms to clean when the family wasn't there.

Each one of our suspects carried a black coat over their arm, some with two. Only Mrs. Gordon, Juliette, and Mrs. Buchanan sat. The men, police and staff stood, as did Miss Wheeler, Oscar and I. It was quite a crowd. All expressed relief at seeing the two abducted women safe and sound.

Then the questions began.

"Why are we gathered here?" Mr. Gordon asked. "My neighbors are welcome, of course, but a little warning would have been nice."

"Yes, why us, specifically?" Mr. Kinloch asked. "And why did we need to bring along our coats?" He indicated both of his arms, each draped with a winter coat.

"All will be revealed," Oscar began. "But first, the constables will be searching your coat pockets."

Once again it was Mr. Gordon and Mr. Kinloch who spoke up, asking why that was necessary. Again, Oscar didn't answer. He signaled for the constables to start with Mr. Kinloch.

The pockets of both his coats were empty.

When the constable reached Blackburn, the coachman stepped back, refusing. "I got rights. You cannae make me show ye." He glared at the constable, daring him to attempt to dig through his coat pockets.

"He can't, but I can, if you want to keep your job," Mr. Kinloch snapped.

Blackburn's nostrils flared.

"Just show him and get it over with. If you're innocent, you have nothing to fear."

Blackburn hesitated then finally gave in. The constable rummaged through the pockets of the coachman's greatcoat then shook his head and moved on to Jack.

The footman shouldered the constable out of the way and ran.

"Stop him!" Miss Wheeler cried.

Mr. Gordon and Redmayne both lunged, but Jack was too nimble for them. Their efforts were unnecessary, as Oscar had remained by the door when the constables left their positions there. He stopped the footman with a well-timed kick at Jack's leg that tripped him, followed by a punch to the gut.

The footman fell to the floor with a thud, howling in pain as he grabbed his leg.

One of the constables stood over him while the other snatched Jack's coat and rummaged through the pockets. I was more interested in the flash of metal I'd seen in the commotion.

"You won't find anything," I told them. "Jack's not involved."

Everyone looked at me.

"How do you know?" Mr. Kinloch asked.

"You know who it is, don't you?" Oscar said. "Go on, Gavin. Who are the kidnappers?"

"I only know one, but I suspect we can easily find out the other two. But first, I need to prove it."

"How?" Miss Wheeler asked.

I opened the door and spoke quietly to Anderson, the Gordons' butler, hovering nearby.

CHAPTER 15

The genuine confusion of our suspects was a clue that my hunch was correct. None knew what we were looking for in their coat pockets, so that meant they hadn't discovered the wool left there by Juliette during her ordeal. But all the pockets were empty of woolen scraps, even those belonging to Mr. and Mrs. Gordon, which their butler had fetched after I spoke to him. Mrs. Buchanan hadn't brought a warm winter coat to Edinburgh, but I'd already dismissed her as a suspect. Not only was she not in the city at the time of the abductions, she was genuinely happy and relieved to see her daughter.

The constables confirmed they found no wool scraps after checking all the coats. That meant someone had removed the wool. And if it wasn't one of our suspects themselves, it had to be someone else. And I knew who.

I was about to explain when Detective Inspector Smith walked in. He'd arrived by carriage with two more constables. He strolled in since the front door wasn't locked. He was relieved to see Juliette and Mary and immediately peppered them with questions. It was Juliette who put up her hand for him to stop.

"Professor Nash was just about to tell us who one of the three kidnappers is," she said. "Professor?"

I briefly recounted what we knew about the kidnappers, including the ownership of the building in which the two women were found, and ending by telling D.I. Smith about Juliette's piece of magic wool. "We've searched all the coat pockets of the suspects and not found it. But that doesn't mean it was never there."

He pointed in the direction of the suspects, all staring back at us with an air of expectation. "It might not be one of these."

"Given the two women were living next door to each other, and Miss Buchanan hasn't been here long, its likely to be someone nearby who has heard about their magic. The male servants from Mary's household all have alibis. Anyway, I don't believe there's any need to widen our search, especially since I now know who did it."

"Because of the wool? But you didn't find it in any pockets."

"The wool is one clue, but there's another that I've just discovered. Or perhaps that should be rediscovered."

"Please, Professor," Mrs. Buchanan urged. "Just tell us." She sat next to her daughter on the sofa, her hand clasping Juliette's. On her other side, Mrs. Gordon sat quite close, a look of utter dismay on her face.

She knew.

Her reaction meant I was right, and knowing that spurred me on. Indeed, I felt invigorated, gripped with a kind of fever similar to the thrill I'd felt when I first read Mr. Kinloch's letter to Lord Coyle regarding George Mackenzie's book. With everyone looking at me, I laid out the evidence.

"The reason we didn't find the wool was because it was removed and thrown away. Not on purpose. The person who removed it didn't know its significance and merely thought it a scrap. He consigned it to the wastebasket."

"'He?'" Oscar echoed.

I nodded at the Gordons' butler.

Anderson's eyes widened. "It wasn't me!"

"I know you're not one of the kidnappers," I assured him. "But you emptied the pocket of a person who is."

"Butlers don't empty coat pockets," Redmayne pointed out with all the snooty aloofness I'd come to expect from him. "That's the job for a valet. Or the maid, serving the ladies of the house."

"In wealthy households that's true. But in financial difficulty, sometimes housekeepers act as lady's maids, and butlers perform the duties of a footman and valet." I indicated the ordinary, mismatched furniture, the lack of heirlooms and knickknacks found in most houses of quality.

"We are not poor," Mrs. Gordon blurted out. "We choose to live simply, as God intended."

"Your butler informed me before he went to fetch your

coats that he has been acting as Mr. Gordon's valet." I turned to Anderson. The poor man looked like a fish caught on the end of a hook. Despite my sympathy for his predicament, I couldn't soften my questions now. "You found a thread of wool in a coat pocket on the day Juliette was abducted, didn't you? Would you mind telling us whose coat you found it in?"

Mrs. Gordon shot to her feet. "No! Don't answer that."

Anderson's mouth opened and shut without uttering a word.

"Never mind," I said. "You may want to confide in D.I. Smith after I tell you what the second piece of evidence is." I crossed the room to the fireplace and rested a hand on the white marble mantelpiece. "Juliette and Mary were kept in a hidden room that was accessed by pressing a carved escutcheon on the mantelpiece. It was larger than my hand and positioned in a row of similar images." I held out my hand as I strolled past some of the standing suspects. It was a piece of theater but I was pleased to see them all study the size of my hand. "At the time, I thought the stonemason had carved the original owner's clan crest into the stone, and didn't think it relevant. But I now know it *is* relevant. Perhaps the stag head used to represent a particular clan. Now, however, it represents a secret society. A dangerous one." I stopped in front of Mr. Gordon and pointed at the gold pin on his lapel. "It's the same as that."

Mr. Gordon scoffed as he rocked back on his heels. "Stags are common representations here in Scotland. This pin represents my club."

"What sort of club?" I asked.

Mr. Gordon sniffed. "I'm not answering you."

I felt Oscar move up behind me. His presence gave me strength to continue. "It's not a *gentleman's* club, is it? There's at least one female member. It's probably more accurate to describe it as a secret sect. Tell me, is the sect led by a practicing vicar? Or did he leave the church and start his own, more secretive, sinister faith when his fire-and-brimstone preaching became too much for his parishioners?"

It was a leap, but one I suspected would get a response. Just as I'd hoped, Mrs. Gordon shot to her feet again.

"It's not a sect! Tell them, my dear. Tell them he's wrong. He must be!" She pressed a hand to her chest. "He must be wrong. Juliette is our niece."

Mr. Gordon met my gaze with a defiant one of his own. "This is absurd. It's all nonsense. So I have a pin that looks similar to a carving in a mantelpiece in an old building. It means nothing."

Instead of replying, I turned to Anderson. "You've been acting as valet to Mr. Gordon. The task involves taking care of his clothing. When you brushed down his winter coat, you checked the pockets as a matter of course. On the day Juliette went missing, you probably thought it odd that he'd been out in summer wearing a winter coat, but then you dismissed it from your mind. While cleaning Mr. Gordon's coat, you removed a piece of wool from his pocket. What color was it?" I'd not yet told them the color of the wool. Few in that room knew it came from the head of Juliette's favorite doll as a child.

The butler swallowed heavily and glanced at Mr. Gordon. Mr. Gordon glared back at him. It was full of threatening malice.

D.I. Smith pointed out a rather obvious fact to Anderson. "If you don't tell the truth, you'll be charged with aiding the kidnappers."

"It was pale yellow," Anderson said on a rush of breath.

Mrs. Buchanan gathered her daughter in her arms and squeezed her eyes shut. Tears slipped from beneath her lashes and down her cheeks. Juliette, meanwhile, glared daggers at her uncle.

He did not look her way. "This is vindictive, nasty and demonstrably false. You'll be dismissed over this, Detective."

"It can be verified," Oscar said. "He fired a gun at us outside the building where Juliette and Mary were held prisoner. The bullet lodged in the wall will match the type of gun in his possession. He would have returned to the house not long ago."

Everyone looked to Anderson. The butler nodded grimly.

D.I. Smith sent two of his men off to search the house for the gun. "Do you know the address of the building where the women were held?"

Mary gave it to him. "We reckon the vicar who owns it is the one who did all the talking. Real madman, he was, always going on about us being abominations, saying if we admitted we were witches we could repent and be clean again to receive God's love in Heaven. Miss Buchanan reckoned he was going tae kill us if we admitted it." The maid folded her arms over her chest, hugging herself.

Juliette rose and drew Mary into an embrace. "It's all over now, Mary. We're safe."

Mrs. Buchanan stood too, but not to be with her daughter. She wanted to get away from her sister-in-law, still seated on the sofa. "You should be ashamed of yourself."

"I didn't know," Mrs. Gordon whispered.

"You must have known. Is the vicar from your kirk?"

Mrs. Gordon gave a slight nod. "He was originally from Edinburgh, but served in Glasgow for over a decade. The bishop moved him on in January after complaints from some parishioners. His new parish here in Edinburgh didn't work out either, so he resigned. He called on some of his former parishioners, saying he wanted to continue his brand of faith with a few like-minded devotees. I declined to join, but..." Her gaze lifted to her husband, standing still as a statue in the middle of the room. "But my husband followed him."

Mr. Gordon suddenly came to life again. "I don't believe in that nonsense. I never have. The vicar is from an old and wealthy family. He owns a great deal of property in his own right." He jutted his chin forward and tugged on his sleeves. "I found myself in need of money after an investment I made some years ago turned sour." He shot a glare at Mr. Kinloch. "I asked the vicar for a loan, and he agreed as long as I helped him cleanse the city of witches. It was all his idea, the kidnappings, the ridiculous straw effigies as a warning that we were coming for the rest of the witches... I simply did as he bade me to secure the loan."

"You kidnapped your own niece!" Mrs. Buchanan cried. "What would you have done if she admitted to being a witch in front of the vicar? Would you have killed her if she confessed?"

Mr. Gordon flinched as if he'd been slapped, but that was the only sign he gave of having heard her. "I couldn't control the vicar. He's a madman. He blackmailed me into helping him. I'm a victim, too."

Mrs. Buchanan stepped forward and did slap him, right across the cheek. Going by the sound and the mark left behind, it had been hard. "You're pathetic," she growled at him. "Take responsibility for your actions instead of blaming others."

Mr. Gordon bristled and opened his mouth to protest, but he didn't get the opportunity to speak.

Redmayne stepped up and punched Mr. Gordon in the stomach. The gentleman doubled over, coughing and clutching his middle. We all stared at Redmayne.

He glared at Mr. Gordon, who was struggling to regain the breath that had been knocked out of him. "It was you! *You* kidnapped and murdered my Dorothy."

Good lord, he was right. It had to have been Mr. Gordon. His wife was friends with Mrs. Carter, the former employer of Redmayne and his lover. Mrs. Carter must have told Mrs.

Gordon that her maid was boasting about being a cotton magician, and Mrs. Gordon went home and told her husband. He kidnapped her, extracting a confession from her. Then he killed her to cleanse the city of a witch, as he'd called it. Indeed, it was the motive he'd assigned to the vicar.

But the vicar wasn't behind that particular abduction. He couldn't have been. He wasn't yet working in the local parish. According to Mrs. Gordon, he'd been in Glasgow at the time of that abduction.

She realized, too. Her face paled. The hand she raised to cover her mouth shook.

I had one more question to ask. "Mary, Miss Buchanan, when did you last see or hear the woman during your ordeal?"

"She came this morning to give us breakfast." Juliette's gaze flicked to her aunt and back to me. "I don't think it was *her*."

"She was with me all morning," Mrs. Buchanan said. "From the moment I got out of bed she's been comforting me." Her gaze softened a little, but she didn't go to her sister-in-law. I wondered if she'd ever be ready to renew the family bond that connected them.

Mrs. Gordon gave no indication that she realized we were talking about her. She'd reverted to a state of stupor, her gaze distant and somewhat vacant. Her fingers clasped the cross brooch at her throat so tightly that she might rip it off the collar.

"I'll find the woman," the detective assured us. "If

Gordon doesn't confess, I can easily find out the name of the former vicar who owns that building, and I've got ways of getting people to give up their associates." One of his constables cracked his knuckles, earning an audible gulp from Mr. Gordon.

Two constables manhandled Mr. Gordon out of the room. His hair was in disarray, and he was still bent forward in pain from the punch. He didn't utter a word in his defense. He must have realized it was hopeless.

Mary took a moment to thank Juliette again for being strong throughout the ordeal, and for stopping her confessing to their captors. Staying silent saved her life. Agnes circled an arm around Mary then steered her from the room. For all her previous spitefulness over Mary's flirting, she was being kind to her now.

Jack also limped out, taking his coat with him. He seemed eager to go. I couldn't blame him. It occurred to me that Mr. Gordon had written those love letters to his own niece. It was possible the vicar or the woman had written them, I supposed. Whoever did, poor Jack the footman had been unwittingly dragged into the plot. A part of me felt compelled to go after him to offer words of comfort, but I hesitated so long that the opportunity vanished.

Redmayne and Blackburn followed him out. Mr. Kinloch lingered to speak to us.

"If you haven't already guessed, Gordon invested in my company," he said. "My wool mill is failing, which is why I'm selling my art collection, among other things. I am partly to blame for his actions. I feel awful."

Several voices disagreed with his harsh opinion of himself, but Mrs. Buchanan's was loudest. "You are not to blame. Not in the least."

"My company makes textiles, and magicians of the same discipline as Juliette and Mary are the reason behind its failure. Well, that and the fact I haven't given the business the attention it needs. I've been too busy with my distillery. Whiskey is my passion, you see, not wool."

"What if someone else managed it for you?" Miss Wheeler asked with a sly smile. "Someone who may lack business skills but is clever enough to pick it up and also has a knack for wool?" Her gaze slid to Juliette.

Juliette looked to her mother. "Can I?"

Mrs. Buchanan laughed. "Don't ask me, ask Mr. Kinloch."

Mr. Kinloch paused then thrust out his hand. "I think we can work something out. We'll discuss the particulars when you're feeling up to it. By the way, do you think Mary would be interested, too? Wool-cotton blends are the way of the future."

"I'll ask her." Juliette darted off toward the door.

Mrs. Buchanan smiled at Mr. Kinloch. "Thank you. This will be good for her. The idle life of a lady isn't for her."

Mr. Kinloch gave a shallow bow of acknowledgment. "Perhaps seeing their cheerful faces every day at the office is just the thing to get me interested in that business again. Their faces, *and* yours, dear lady, if I may be so bold."

Mrs. Buchanan smiled softly. "We'll see." Her smile vanished as she caught sight of her sister-in-law, still seated on the sofa. "I'll remain in Edinburgh for some time, so we'll certainly be seeing more of each other, Mr. Kinloch."

He bowed again. "I look forward to some neighborly interactions."

We walked from the room with him, and Anderson saw us out. The journalist we'd seen lounging against the garden fence earlier was back. He scribbled furiously in his notebook as Blackburn spoke to him. Mr. Kinloch didn't seem to mind that his coachman was going to earn a little extra on the side by talking to the press.

At his front steps, he turned to us and shook each of our hands in turn. "I was glad to sell *A Treatise on the Laws of Witchcraft and Maleficium in Scotland* to you Professor. I knew you would be worthy. Now I'm doubly glad. Triply! Thank you for bringing those women back safely. All of you."

A hollow pit opened in my gut. I felt guilty for not telling him it had been stolen. I felt even more guilty that I still considered him a suspect for the theft. But I didn't want to accuse him now. It didn't feel right. If he needed the money so desperately, he should keep the book and resell it.

We said our goodbyes and continued on. Mr. Kinloch was right. We'd done a wonderful thing today. It was growing late and I was hungry and exhausted. I'd probably fall asleep in my room again, but this time I wouldn't leave anything valuable out for anyone to steal.

"Miss Wheeler, will you join us in the hotel's private dining room this evening to celebrate?" Oscar asked.

"Mr. Defoe wouldn't like that," she said.

"Forget Defoe then." From the enthusiastic way he looked at her, I wondered if he'd say to forget me next. Oscar was quite smitten.

She laughed lightly. "I can't. Besides, he'll probably want to leave as soon as I return."

"Is there a London train this evening?"

"We're not going to London."

Oscar sighed. "Pity. I was looking forward to spending several hours with you."

"We wouldn't have sat together, Mr. Barratt. Mr. Defoe wouldn't like that. He's very bitter about losing the Mackenzie book to you and will be for a long time."

"Speaking of which," Oscar said mildly, "may we have it back?"

CHAPTER 16

"Oscar!" I cried. "You can't accuse Miss Wheeler without evidence!"

"That's a fair point, and ordinarily I wouldn't. But I do have good instincts, and in this case, my instincts have served me well."

I pushed my glasses up my nose to study Miss Wheeler. She was unmoved by the accusation. "Is he right?"

She stopped and rested the point of her umbrella into the groove between pavement stones. She folded her hands over the top and regarded me levelly. "He is. I am sorry, Professor."

"Why did you take it?"

"To get you involved in finding the missing women. I saw the newspaper headlines at the station when we arrived in Edinburgh, then I read the article at Kinloch's while you were all negotiating the sale of the book. I couldn't sleep that night thinking about them. The article mentioned witchcraft, and given I am a woman and a magician...it felt very personal. Considering most police forces around the world lack time and resources, I suspected Edinburgh's could do with some help from three enterprising, clever people. I doubted you'd change your plans on a whim to take on an investigation that had nothing to do with you, so I gave you an incentive, as it were."

She'd picked the lock on my hotel room door! She'd used her hairpins, just as she'd done with the door to the building where the captives were being held. "You left the straw effigy in place of the book to make us think the theft was linked to the kidnappings."

"I read about them in the newspaper, but I didn't get it quite right, as the police pointed out when we showed it to them." She reached out and clasped my hand. "I am sorry for manipulating you, Professor."

"I don't understand. What made you think we were enterprising and clever? You'd only just met us."

"I could tell as soon as I met you that you were a quick thinker, Professor. I underestimated you, however. Your mind could best be described as formidable. The way you deduced that it was Mr. Gordon was marvelous."

I lowered my head, but I doubted I managed to hide my blushing cheeks from her.

She was polite enough not to point it out. "Can you forgive my duplicitousness, Professor?" She squeezed my hand.

I squeezed back. "Of course I can. The outcome is beyond wonderful."

She breathed deeply and a look of relief washed over her. She squeezed my hand again before releasing it. "Just one more thing. Mr. Defoe doesn't know that I took the book, and I prefer that he doesn't find out. I especially don't want him finding out that I gave it back to you."

Oscar and I assured her he wouldn't learn anything from us.

We resumed walking, Miss Wheeler between Oscar and me. "You are wrong about one thing," Oscar told her, his voice low, as if he wanted only her to hear, no one else. Not even me. "We would have changed our plans to help you. All you needed to do was ask."

She blinked rapidly in an attempt to hide the emotion suddenly welling in her eyes. "Thank you, Mr. Barratt."

"Please call me Oscar."

She drew in a deep breath and let it out slowly, her emotions once more under control. "No."

He chuckled.

We continued at a leisurely pace back to the hotel, none of us in a hurry to return to Defoe and what must be the end for this new friendship. Despite that, I felt full. I was in the company of two people I liked and admired, I'd solved a mystery, and ushered two young women back into the arms of their loved ones. I was also about to get the book back. To add to my good mood, the clouds parted, revealing a lovely blue sky. Afternoon sunlight bathed the honey-colored buildings in a warm glow to match the warm glow within me. The city hummed with activity, but at a gentler pace compared to London, and the air wasn't nearly as smelly or thick. All was right with the world again.

* * *

AFTER CHANGING my shirt for a fresh one, I joined Oscar in his room. It was too early for dinner, but we hoped to find a tavern or inn for refreshments. I watched as he tied his tie in the reflection of the dressing table mirror. I couldn't tell if he was happy or forlorn. He seemed thoughtful, his mind not quite on the task at hand. He made a mess of the knot.

"You can't go out like that," I chided.

He pulled a face at his reflection. "You're right." He turned to me. "Can you do it?"

I undid the tie and restarted. "When did you know Miss Wheeler took the book?"

"I had an inkling when we confronted Defoe this morning. I believed his denial, but I couldn't think who else might have taken it. She seemed the logical choice, but I'm ashamed to say I dismissed the idea simply because I couldn't imagine a woman breaking into your room in the night. When the police told us our effigy was different, I realized the theft probably wasn't connected to the abductions at all, then throughout the day, I slowly began to realize it must be her. When she unlocked that door in the close, I knew it for certain. Did it never occur to you she'd taken it to encourage us to investigate the abductions?"

"Not once. It still seems an extreme method when she could have just asked."

"She couldn't be sure we would agree."

I finished tying his tie and stepped back to make sure it was straight.

Oscar cleared his throat. "She was right, Gavin. You were magnificent today."

"I didn't find Juliette and Mary. Miss Wheeler did that with her chalk dust."

"You found the way to open the hidden door, and you were the one who worked out Gordon was the culprit then went on to prove it. I knew your big brain would come in useful on these jaunts." His eyes twinkled with his smile. "It seems I was the superfluous one of the trio."

"Hardly. You're the glue."

"Thank you." I wasn't sure if he was thanking me for calling him the glue or for tying his tie.

"I must apologize for getting carried away in the Gordons' drawing room," I said. "I don't know what came over me, but laying out the evidence to everyone, and finally putting it all together and unmasking Mr. Gordon… it was all rather invigorating."

"I could see you were enjoying yourself."

"Could you? Oh. That makes me sound thoughtless, given the awful circumstances."

"Don't worry. I'm probably the only one who noticed."

A knock at the door had Oscar rushing eagerly to open it. "Miss Wheeler, do come in. Gavin is here."

She looked past him and lifted a hand in a wave. In it, she held the book. "Take it quickly. Mr. Defoe will be here any moment."

Oscar accepted it and handed it to me without even glancing at it. "Leave him, Adele." He grasped her hand between both of his. "Leave Defoe and come with us."

She plucked out her hand. "Thank you for the offer, but I decline. Again."

"May I write to you?"

"You may not." She turned her head to the side, listening, as Mr. Defoe arrived. "Also, it's Miss Wheeler to you."

Mr. Defoe chuckled. "Give up, Barratt. She'll never be trapped."

Miss Wheeler kept her features schooled. "Goodbye, Mr. Barratt, Professor."

I joined Oscar and held out my hand for her to shake. "Goodbye, Miss Wheeler. Mr. Defoe."

She removed her hand from mine and offered it to Oscar. "I want to apologize for calling you an idiot after the second shooting. You're not an idiot. Indeed, you're far from it. In fact, you're not a bad fellow."

"Not bad?" He smiled slyly. "You do recall the way I stopped Jack the footman escaping from the drawing room, don't you? He's a big fellow."

"Handsome, too," she added, teasing.

"Some would say he's not rough enough around the edges." He scratched his goatee beard.

She rolled her eyes.

"Take the compliment, Barratt," Mr. Defoe chimed in. "She doesn't hand them out often." He withdrew his watch from his waistcoat pocket and made a point of checking the time. "Come, Adele, we have a train to catch."

"Goodbye, Mr. Barratt," she said, tugging her hand to withdraw it from his.

Oscar lifted it to his lips. "Not goodbye," he murmured against the glove. "I have a strong feeling we'll meet again."

Her gaze met his. Whatever she saw in his eyes unnerved her. She swallowed heavily and snatched her hand free. She picked up her umbrella, which she'd rested against the wall and joined Mr. Defoe. The gentleman touched the brim of his hat in farewell, offered his assistant his arm, and they headed off along the corridor.

Oscar watched them until they turned the corner, but Miss Wheeler did not look back. With a sigh, he closed the door.

I quickly checked the book to ensure it hadn't incurred any damage and no pages had been torn out. While I trusted Miss Wheeler implicitly, I did not trust her employer. He may have found the book among her belongings while she was out investigating with us. It was in the same condition as the last time I'd seen it, thank goodness. I folded it against my chest and released a sigh that was more satisfied than Oscar's disappointed one.

The last time I'd seen Oscar this smitten, he'd proposed

to Lady Louisa. Before that, he'd been enamored of India Steele. Perhaps it was time to point out a sobering fact about Miss Wheeler to help him overcome this new infatuation before it ate away at him.

"She took advantage of us, Oscar. She knew you liked her, and that I would follow where you led, and she used that to manipulate us. Granted, her manipulations were for a good purpose, but the fact is, only a certain type of person does that."

"One who is desperate? She wanted to find those women and she didn't know how else to go about it. She couldn't do it alone and Defoe wasn't going to be of any use. I am happy to be manipulated, in this instance."

It would seem I was too late. He was more infatuated with her than I had realized. That hadn't taken long at all.

Oscar asked for the book, then placed it inside his valise before locking it. "Do you believe in fate, Gavin?"

"No."

"Soulmates?"

"Oscar, you *will* find someone to love. You have a good heart, and I know in my bones you'll find someone worthy to give it to."

"What if I already have?"

I wanted to put a comforting arm around him, but wasn't sure how he'd react, so I tilted my head to the side and gave him a sympathetic look. "I mean someone who is available. Miss Wheeler has made it clear she is not."

He picked up his hat and twirled it. "That's not the message I got."

"She told you not to write to her."

"But her eyes said something quite different."

"If you can read eyes so well then read these." I lifted my glasses and rolled my eyes in such an exaggerated manner that it hurt my eyeballs. "Ow."

Oscar chuckled and placed his arm around my shoulders. "Come on. I need a drink."

"A cup of tea would do nicely."

"I was thinking of something stronger. Let's see if we can find a place that stocks Kinloch's whiskey."

* * *

THE SWAYING MOTION of the train didn't affect me as much on the journey back to London as it had on the way up to Edinburgh. I suspected it was because I felt less anxious. Our first expedition had come to an end, and I'd proved to myself that I was capable. Being away from the familiar comforts of home wasn't as terrifying as I'd thought it would be.

That was most likely because of the capable and fearless man sitting opposite me. Oscar finally closed *A Treatise on the Laws of Witchcraft and Maleficium in Scotland* as we pulled into King's Cross Station. After his disappointment over the parting with Miss Wheeler, I let him read the book first to cheer him up. It seemed to have the desired effect, going by the secretive little smile he sported.

"Well?" I prompted.

"It's an interesting book, once you get past the archaic

spelling and terminology. Mackenzie's thoughts on witchcraft are remarkably modern by the standards of his time." Oscar's lips flattened. "Mr. Gordon's secret sect notwithstanding."

The similarities of the circumstances surrounding the abductions of Juliette and Mary to the persecution of witches in the seventeenth century, when the book was written, had given me much to think about on the journey. While a great deal had changed over the centuries, there were pockets of society that hadn't. Thankfully, nowadays it was the witchfinders who were imprisoned, not the so-called witches they hunted.

Oscar's small smile returned, so he mustn't be thinking about the topic of witchcraft. Only two things could produce that smile and Miss Wheeler was one of them. Since she and Mr. Defoe had left Edinburgh last night for parts unknown, I guessed it was the other matter that made him happy.

"You found the reference to the tattoo." I indicated the book, opened to a page near the end on his lap.

He turned it around to show me and pointed at a paragraph. "Mackenzie heard a story about a tattoo that makes a person fly when they speak a spell. He uses the term witch, but we can assume it's an ink magician."

I read the paragraph then glanced up at Oscar. His eyes were feverishly bright, his smile barely contained. "We're going to Italy next, aren't we?"

His smile finally broke free. "We are. But first, we need to deliver this to India and Matt."

CHAPTER 17

"I'm coming with you next time." The declaration was made by Willie's friend, Lord Farnsworth. The lackadaisical dandy lounged on Lord and Lady Rycroft's sofa, much like Mr. Defoe had done on Mr. Kinloch's. Whereas Defoe's pose had been arrogant, Farnsworth's was more refined, as befitted the cultured accent and expensive education. When I'd first met him, I'd thought he was putting on the foppish air to make people think he was harmlessly eccentric, but the more I got to know him, the less certain my opinion of him became. He was definitely more intelligent than he let on, but the lurid waistcoats, diamond cufflinks, and pompous languor were as much a part of him as Willie's loud unruliness was a part of her.

"No, you ain't," she said. "*I'm* going next time."

"You can't," Lord Farnsworth said. "You're married."

"So?"

"Your husband'll want you home, making babies and playing hostess."

Everyone burst out laughing, including Detective Inspector Brockwell, the husband in question. We sat in the drawing room of number sixteen Park Street, the London residence of Lord and Lady Rycroft, where Willie and Brockwell currently resided. Aside from Matt and India, Willie, Brockwell and Farnsworth, we were joined by their friend, Duke, and Matt's elderly aunt, Miss Letitia Glass. She sat in a chair by the window, her head bowed forward as she napped. She wasn't the only one asleep. Young Gabriel, the Rycrofts' son, was having an afternoon nap in his room, allowing the adults to have an uninterrupted conversation.

I used the term *adult* loosely when it came to Willie and Lord Farnsworth. They could each be as disruptive as a toddler sometimes, especially when they were together.

"You won't go," Duke said to Willie. His thick fingers looked unnaturally large as he gripped the teacup like it was the handle of a hammer. He waved it in Willie's general direction. "You won't leave Matt."

"Or little Gabe," D.I. Brockwell added, not in the least upset that his wife placed her cousins above him in her affections.

Willie bristled, but instead of disagreeing she sipped her tea. Her silence made quite a stark contrast to the battle of wills she usually exhibited with Duke ever since he revealed he was returning to America.

We'd joined India and Matt for afternoon tea, and to

present them with the book, two days after our arrival back in London. The lull in the conversation gave Oscar the perfect opportunity. He removed it from the leather satchel at his feet and handed it to India.

"For your collection, my lady." He bowed, stepped forward to give it to her, then stepped back.

India stroked the soft calfskin cover. "Thank you. Have either of you read it?"

"We both have," Oscar said.

"What's it about?" Willie asked.

"Observations on magic, or witchcraft, as the author, George Mackenzie called it. He also touches on the persecution of witches at that time."

"Thank goodness that has all ended," India murmured.

I sat forward. "Actually, we learned that it hasn't. Our time in Edinburgh was more interesting and productive than we expected. You see, we rescued—"

Matt shushed me with a finger to his lips as his aunt roused in the armchair.

Miss Glass reminded me of my grandmother, whose death seven years ago had shaken me. Both women were kind but could be snobs, too. My grandmother welcomed my friendships with university chums from good families, but she didn't want me associating with people she thought beneath us. Considering we Nashes were firmly embedded in the middle class, her snobbery wasn't justified. At least Miss Glass could claim to be from nobility.

As with my grandmother, Miss Glass had become quite forgetful in her later years. I saw her rarely these days, since she usually stayed on the country estate, but I had noticed a decline in her cognition. She sometimes didn't know where she was, or who I was, and she found conversations hard to follow.

Then sometimes, like now, she could surprise us all and be quite alert. "Did someone say Edinburgh? Bristow says the newspapers reported those missing girls were found. Isn't that wonderful?"

India pretended to refill my teacup, leaning closer to me. "Tell us how you did it later," she whispered, adding a wink for good measure.

While Miss Glass was aware of some of the dangers her nephew and his wife had endured to free magicians from persecution, she was sheltered from other events. It would seem they wanted to continue to shelter her from negativity in her dotage.

"Wonderful, indeed," India said loudly as she sat. "The Edinburgh police must have an equivalent to D.I. Brockwell on their staff."

Brockwell winked at me, just as India had done. I wasn't sure if that meant he hadn't told any of them that the Edinburgh detective contacted him to vouch for us, or if he was withholding the information from Miss Glass alone.

Willie didn't make it any clearer. "Nope. My husband's one of a kind. Ain't no detective as good as him."

Oscar shot me a sly smile. "I can think of someone."

I felt my face heat at his praise. To deflect their attention from me, I changed the subject to one that would draw the energy in the room like a magnet. I turned to Willie. "I see you've come to terms with Duke leaving."

True to form, Willie sank into her chair with a pout and crossed her arms. "I'll never come to terms with it. He shouldn't be going. There ain't nothing for him in America now."

Duke waved a hand from side to side. "Ain't no need to speak to me as if I'm not here."

"I thought you two sorted it out over drinks," Oscar said.

"I thought we had, too. Then she stopped talking to me. She's going to ruin my final weeks in England with her bad mood." His gaze slid to Miss Glass. "Willie's not the only one who dislikes the idea of me leaving."

Miss Glass seemed unaware that he was referring to her. She sat in the chair, her glassy eyes staring at the floor near my feet.

Oscar pointed at the book India had placed on the table. "George Mackenzie wrote about the unfair treatment of women accused of witchcraft back in his day. Their persecution took away their freedom, their right to be true to themselves."

Willie narrowed her gaze. "Your point, Barratt?"

"Those two kidnapped women were elated and relieved to be freed from captivity. Their loved ones were overjoyed, too. So I imagine," he added for Miss Glass's benefit, although she still seemed not to be listening. "Giving someone the freedom to live their life as they wish is the greatest gift we can offer our loved ones. Even if that means we have to say goodbye to them."

Willie sniffed as she turned her face away. Her jaw remained stubbornly firm.

Miss Glass put out her hand. "Duke, help me up."

He obliged, assisting her to her feet. The contrast between them was stark. Her clothing hung loose on her thin frame, the black silk bringing out the gray pallor of her cheeks. It suddenly occurred to me that she knew Duke's departure meant she'd never see him again.

But it was Duke who blinked back tears as she tilted her head to look up at him.

"Mr. Barratt is right," Miss Glass said, her voice as frail as her frame. "I give you my blessing, Duke. May you find what you're looking for in America."

He bent to kiss her cheek. "I promise I'll write every week, although I don't reckon my words will be as pretty as Barratt's."

Oscar nodded thoughtfully. "It was quite a rousing speech. Gavin, will you write it into your travel diary for me so I don't forget it?"

Duke helped Miss Glass sit again, then released her just in time so he could catch Willie as she flung herself at him. She wrapped her arms around him and buried her face in his chest. I suspected she was silently crying, but it wasn't until she lifted her head that I saw the evidence of tears on her cheeks.

She poked his shoulder. "I give you my blessing, too. You can go and find yourself a nice wife in America and have babies with her. But I expect one of them to be named Willie."

Duke laughed. "I knew there'd be a condition." He hugged her fiercely.

Lord Farnsworth removed a crisp white handkerchief from his pocket with a flourish and dabbed at his eyes. "Am I happy or sad?" He flapped the handkerchief in front of his face. "I can't tell!"

We talked a while longer, until it was time for us to leave. Oscar and I had someone else to call on before the day was over. As we said our goodbyes, Oscar asked India how her grandfather, Chronos, fared.

"The same," she said, a measure of resignation in her voice. "The doctor says there isn't anything to be done. We can only make sure he's comfortable. We're returning to Rycroft Hall tomorrow to be with him."

Oscar patted her hand in sympathy then kissed her cheek, under the close scrutiny of her husband. He then shook Matt's hand. "I'll send through our account of expenses. You'll be pleasantly surprised at the price we paid for that book."

We all looked at the copy of *A Treatise on the Laws of Witchcraft and Maleficium in Scotland* by His Majesty's Lord Advocate George Mackenzie. It was an insignificant looking volume for such a seminal work.

Matt placed an arm around India and tucked her against his side. "It'll be a worthy addition to the collection."

She placed a hand over his at her waist. "You'll be

pleased to know that Lord Coyle's collection had some real gems in it, Professor. They're currently in the attic. You can come and read them at any time." She gazed up at her husband who smiled back at her. "Taking possession of Coyle's books feels like a final ending, as if we've turned the page of the last chapter and there's no more of the story. It's a relief. Although we will see Hope and Valentine at family events from time to time."

Willie made a sound of disgust in her throat, but refrained from commenting.

She, Farnsworth, and Brockwell walked outside with us. "Join Willie and me for a chop later?" Brockwell asked. "Let's say eight at Ye Olde Cheshire Cheese. I want to hear how you found those girls."

Willie nudged Farnsworth in the ribs. "He really just wants a report on his Edinburgh counterparts. The stupider you can make them seem, Barratt, the better."

"I'm coming for a drink, too," Lord Farnsworth piped up. "You know I like these rambunctious inns you find, Willie. They're full of interesting folk." His face brightened. "We can plan the next book-hunting expedition. I think we should go to Transylvania."

Willie rolled her eyes. "Ignore Davide. He likes the gothic penny dreadfuls. I reckon we should go to America. We can help Duke settle in while we're there."

"He can settle in on his own," Brockwell said gently. He put one arm around her waist, as Matt had done with India, and kissed her cheek, knocking her hat askew in the process.

She removed it altogether and leaned into him.

"We've already decided on Italy," I told them.

"And neither of you are coming with us," Oscar added.

A hansom cab pulled up alongside us, carrying a familiar passenger. I stumbled in surprise at the sight of her and felt quite foolish about it when Oscar remained composed. After all, he should be more startled than me at the sudden appearance of his former fiancée.

"Bloody hell," he muttered under his breath. Louder, he said, "What are you doing here?"

Lady Louisa looked as pretty as always in a green-and-white-striped waistcoat over a white chemise. Her fair hair was artfully arranged in ringlets that framed her face, giving her an almost childlike appearance. She crooked a gloved finger, beckoning him to approach the carriage. He did not, so she got out and approached him.

"May we speak in private, Oscar?"

Brockwell steered Willie away, much to her irritation, and Lord Farnsworth trotted along after them. I remained, since Oscar and I had another call to make, but I gave them space. Not so much space that I couldn't hear their exchange, however.

I watched on as Louisa grasped Oscar's hands between both of hers and gave them an imploring shake. "Oscar, I need to speak with you."

He pulled free. "I have no wish to rehash our relationship, Louisa."

"Is that why you haven't answered my letters?"

"I've been away." He sounded as though he was going

to leave it there, but added, "Even so, I wasn't going to respond. It's over between us. It has been for some time. We've both moved on. You're married, so I hear."

She winced and folded her arms across her stomach. "We rushed into it. I should never..." She shook her head.

"You should never have chosen a husband purely because he's a magician?" Oscar gave a hollow laugh. "We all warned you, Louisa."

"He's a good husband. At least, he tries to be. But I don't love him. I still have feelings for you." She suddenly reached for his hands again. "My affection for you is stronger than ever."

He removed his hands and stepped back. "I'm sorry, but any lingering feelings I harbored for you have now completely vanished. Go back to your husband, or don't. I don't care. Goodbye, Louisa. Don't try to contact me again."

"Is there someone else?" she called out as he walked away.

She couldn't see his smile, but I could. "Yes."

"Who?"

He didn't answer. He joined me and we continued walking. I glanced back to see Louisa climbing into the cab. "That encounter helped prepare me for our next port of call," Oscar said. "How about you?"

***

I wasn't ready to visit Lady Coyle, but I never would be. She was as hospitable as a rainy day at the park. This visit was even worse than the last one, thanks to the noise and activity. The noise came from her son, Valentine, crying somewhere in the house. The activity came from men removing her furniture.

"Selling a few more things?" Oscar asked, casually.

"It's none of your business." She stood in the middle of the empty entrance hall, chewing on a thumbnail as two men struggled to carry a large armoire across the tiles.

"It's not a voluntary sale, then."

Her icy glare slid to him. "What do you want?"

"We want to tell you what a low act it was to notify Defoe about the book in Kinloch's possession. You knew we'd try to purchase it from him after reading his letter to your husband."

"You've said your piece, now leave." She strode to the door, a signal for us to exit.

Upstairs, Valentine's crying got louder. Lady Coyle didn't react. Surely, she heard him. I had a mind to find the child myself. He was clearly in need of comforting. From the angry look on his mother's face, he wasn't going to get any comfort from her.

"We should go," I said quietly to Oscar.

He nodded but didn't move. "I hope Defoe paid you well for your betrayal," he said to Lady Coyle.

"Betrayal?" Lady Coyle scoffed. "I owe you nothing. You and your vile, perverted friend got what you wanted—"

"My *what*?" Oscar bellowed.

"He's one of those men who likes other men. It's obvious to everyone. Are you and he *special* friends?"

I pushed Oscar through the door before he could inflame the situation. He surprised me, however, by offering no resistance.

"Bloody awful woman," he said. "Ignore her, Gavin."

My strides lengthened in my eagerness to get away from Lady Coyle. And from Oscar, too. I couldn't face him, not with my cheeks flaming. I felt hot all over, my collar too tight for my neck. I loathed that my body couldn't control its visceral reactions. Life would be so much easier if my emotions weren't on full display for everyone to witness.

Oscar came up alongside me, as calm as could be. He probably didn't even realize I was rushing. "It doesn't bother me that she thinks you and I are more than friends. Nobody else thinks that. Anyway, she was probably just lashing out because she was angry at her furniture being taken away. Seems she really is struggling financially."

I stayed silent, despite the jumble of responses vying for space in my head.

"It's all right, though." Oscar sounded hesitant. He was rarely hesitant. "It doesn't affect our friendship, nor will it stop us traveling together. Your interest in men doesn't—"

I stopped. Turned. "My what?"

Oscar cleared his throat. He glanced around to make sure no one was within earshot. "Don't worry. Your secret is safe with me. But I do want to make it clear that I'm not interested in you in *that* way."

"You arrogant fool, Oscar!" Out of all the things I could have said—wanted to say—*that* was the first thing that popped out? I should have apologized, but instead I made it worse. "I am not interested in you. I'm not interested in anyone in that way, man or woman."

Instead of being put off by my outburst, Oscar dug in. "You may not be now, but when you meet the right fellow—"

"Stop! You're wrong." I went to walk off, but returned. Now that I'd started, I couldn't hold my tongue, even though my head knew I shouldn't speak my mind. Nothing good ever came of that. But it was as though my thudding heart and rushing blood were pumping the words out of me, and the valve couldn't be closed against the flood. "That's the problem with you, Oscar. You always think you're right."

"Gavin—"

"And another thing. I know why you want the tattoo flying spell. You think it will help you feel powerful and put others in awe of you. You're tired of coming second, losing out to someone else. India chose Matt over you. Louisa chose magical children over you. Miss Wheeler chose Defoe."

"She didn't choose Defoe. She chose freedom and independence. That's a concept I fully support." When I didn't respond, he added, "Now who's the one who thinks he's always right?"

Why was he so calm in the face of my tirade? I felt like a torrent was surging through me. After saying my piece, the torrent had lost some of its power and was now more of a swell. Still, I was discombobulated. My thoughts were disorganized, something I wasn't used to.

I set off at a brisk pace, as much to get away from Oscar as to expend the excess energy coursing through me, so that I could once again think properly. Oscar didn't follow.

After a good walk around Hyde Park, I became very aware that saying my piece changed nothing. In fact, I may have made it worse. Oscar probably thought my outburst was a diversionary tactic to stop him thinking I liked him in *that* way.

Should I address the issue, but with a calmer manner? Or let the matter slide altogether in the hope all would be forgotten?

Considering we were going to travel again in the future, it was probably best that I cleared the air.

I bought a piece of paper at a stationer's shop and wrote a note to Oscar asking him to meet me at the chophouse fifteen minutes before eight so we could talk before the others got there. I handed it to his landlady and asked her to deliver it for me.

I MADE sure I was early for our meeting at Ye Old Cheshire Cheese on Fleet Street. Oscar and I regularly met there, since he was familiar with it from his newspaper days. Its low ceilings, and wood-paneled walls reminded me of my father's study. Even the worn leather upholstered seats and the smell of brandy took me back to the days when I'd sit in the big armchair by the fire and read one of his books while he worked. The clientele made me feel comfortable, too. The literary set often met there to draw inspiration from one another, and educated men discussed theories in dimly lit corners, while journalists boasted loudly about their latest article. Many greeted me with a nod or shake of the hand, a clap on the shoulder or an offer to buy me a drink. I declined them all. I'd spotted Oscar waiting for me.

Although I'd arrived early, he was even earlier. He sat in a booth, two tankards of ale in front of him. He pushed one toward me across the table as I sat opposite.

"Let me begin by apologizing," I said, without a moment's hesitation. Some things shouldn't be delayed, and an apology to my best friend was at the top of that list. "I said some awful things that I regret. I was angry, but that's no excuse."

"It is quite a good excuse." Oscar smiled, but it quickly faded when I didn't return it. "I'm sorry, too, Gavin. I didn't listen to you. I should have let the matter drop."

"Thank you." I touched my tankard against his, then sipped.

Oscar watched me over the rim of his tankard as he sipped, too. "You were right, though. About me. I was going after the tattoo flying spell because of my issue with coming second. It stems back to my childhood and my brother. Isaac is an ink magician, too, but unlike me he has a head for business. That, and being the oldest son, meant he inherited the family ink-manufacturing company. I never wanted it, but perhaps there is some lingering resentment within me still, deep down."

"Oscar," I gently chided. "There's nothing wrong with you. I didn't mean any of what I said."

He set the tankard down and loosely circled it with both hands. "I've been thinking…perhaps we shouldn't go searching for the book with the tattoo flying spell. We'll forget we ever heard about it. We'll look for another book instead. Something less controversial, but important. Another seminal work, like Mackenzie's."

I placed my tankard on the table and tapped my finger on its side. I didn't like seeing him so low, and all because I was embarrassed. I'd had a few hours to mull it over and now knew that it *was* embarrassment that spurred me to lash out, not anger. A part of me wanted to explain further to Oscar, but it wasn't the sort of discussion men had with each other, and certainly not in a chophouse on Fleet Street where we knew three-quarters of the patrons.

"And let Defoe get his hands on the tattoo spell?" I shook my head. "That's even more dangerous than you getting it."

One side of his mouth lifted with his half-smile.

"Besides, I've now got my heart set on an Italian adventure."

The other corner of his mouth joined the first in a relieved smile. He lifted his tankard in salute. "Italy it is."

Willie slid onto the bench seat beside me, knocking my elbow and making the ale spill over the rim of the tankard. She placed an arm around my shoulders. "Celebrating without us?"

"I'm toasting Gavin," Oscar said as D.I. Brockwell sat beside him. "If it wasn't for him, a madman would still be on the loose in Edinburgh."

"Tell me every detail," Brockwell urged.

Willie glanced up as a familiar voice declared in a drunken drawl that he had a salacious piece of gossip about one of the queen's grandsons. "Do it quickly, before Farnsworth gets us all thrown out."

"They won't throw him out," Oscar said. "They'll clamor to buy him another drink to get him talking."

I laughed, and he joined in.

I felt better for having apologized. Now we could both move forward. He may not believe me when I said I had no romantic interest in him, and so we hadn't really resolved the issue, but in a manner befitting well-brought-up Englishmen, we'd repressed it.

For now.

Available 1st September 2026:
BLOODLINES AND BIRTHRIGHT
The Uncensored Memoirs of a Book Hunter #2

Author's Note:

The Lord Advocate George Mackenzie was a real historical figure. Although he authored a number of books, *A Treatise on the Laws of Witchcraft and Maleficium in Scotland* was entirely made up. Another real historical figure, the witch hunter Matthew Hopkins, is also briefly mentioned, but his Scottish counterpart, Thomas Kinloch, is my addition for the purposes of the story.

* * *

Did you know **The Uncensored Memoirs of a Book Hunter** is a spin-off of the **Glass and Steele** series and the **Glass Library** series? Go back to where it all began with book 1, *The Watchmaker's Daughter* by C.J. Archer.

Want to read more of C.J.'s books? As well as historical romantic fantasy, C.J. also writes historical mysteries, light epic fantasy and has some older historical romances that might interest you. Check out her website for descriptions of other books and series and choose one you like.

A MESSAGE FROM THE AUTHOR

I hope you enjoyed reading LAWS OF WITCHCRAFT as much as I enjoyed writing it. As an independent author, getting the word out about my book is vital to its success, so if you liked this book please consider telling your friends and writing a review at the store where you purchased it. If you would like to be contacted when I release a new book, subscribe to my newsletter at http://cjarcher.com/contact-cj/newsletter/.

ALSO BY C.J. ARCHER

SERIES WITH 2 OR MORE BOOKS

The Glass Library

Cleopatra Fox Mysteries

After The Rift

Glass and Steele

The Ministry of Curiosities Series

The Emily Chambers Spirit Medium Trilogy

The 1st Freak House Trilogy

The 2nd Freak House Trilogy

The 3rd Freak House Trilogy

The Assassins Guild Series

Lord Hawkesbury's Players Series

Witch Born

SINGLE TITLES NOT IN A SERIES

The Warrior Priest

Courting His Countess

Surrender

Redemption

The Mercenary's Price

ABOUT THE AUTHOR

C.J. Archer has loved history and books for as long as she can remember and feels fortunate that she found a way to combine the two. She spent her early childhood in the dramatic beauty of outback Queensland, Australia, but now lives in suburban Melbourne with her husband, two children and a mischievous black & white cat named Coco.

Subscribe to C.J.'s newsletter through her website CJARCHER.COM to be notified when she releases a new book, as well as get access to exclusive content. You can also follow her on social media:

facebook.com/CJArcherAuthorPage
instagram.com/authorcjarcher

www.ingramcontent.com/pod-product-compliance
Lightning Source LLC
LaVergne TN
LVHW032202070526
838202LV00007B/277